I0762040

THE TRACKER'S RAGE

INGRID SEYMOUR

PenDreams • BIRMINGHAM

Published by PenDreams
Cover design by "Covers by Juan"

ISBN-13: 9781736061220

CHAPTER 1

Not even two weeks ago I'd learned I was a werewolf. And now, there was more. It seemed I may be an alpha, when all along I'd thought I was an omega.

I shifted my Camaro into fourth, tearing down the highway, headed toward Eric Cross's house. It was past midnight, and traffic was light. I ran two red lights, holding my breath and peering at the rearview mirror, expecting to see flashing lights hot on my tail. But luck was on my side.

My heart pounded in my grip on the steering wheel. The engine roared. Trees and buildings zipped by. The power that propelled me forward made me feel as if I were on a hunt, chasing prey. It filled me with excitement. Though, there was more.

There was also panic.

Eric had told me that alpha's could push their thoughts into the heads of other werewolves, and that they could hear their thoughts back. He had done it to me, had ordered me to run into the woods, to chase him. And I had answered him back. We'd communicated without words, simply through our thoughts.

And then, a few nights ago at the *Pulse Inc.* warehouse, while Blake lay twisting on the floor, in agony with wolfsbane in his veins, I'd felt a terrible pressure in my temples. It had been a familiar sensation. The same one I'd felt with Eric when he talked in my mind, but I hadn't recognized it—not until just moments ago when I'd been sleeping in bed, reliving what had happened through a nightmare. Even in the dream, the same terrible pressure had tormented me until I broke through some mental barrier, and then Blake's voice lanced through my consciousness.

"Stephen, help me!" The words had been loud and clear, and there was no way Blake could have pushed them into my mind. *He* was not an alpha, which meant *I* must be one. But that was impossible!

I shifted gears down as I took a sharp left. The tires screeched against the blacktop.

Still fighting with the realization, I shook my head in denial.

It can't be. It can't be.

It hadn't been but a nightmare, something conjured by my subconscious. There was no way I could have heard Blake's thoughts because only an alpha could have done that, and I was an omega—a weakling. Damien had said so. And if the mage had been wrong, Eric would have mentioned something. He wouldn't have left me in the dark, would he?

The Camaro's engine roared as I accelerated onto Eric's street. I came to an abrupt stop in front of his house, turned the ignition off, jumped out of the car, and ran up the concrete steps to his sliding glass doors. They were closed and didn't open for me as usual. But he wasn't expecting me for a training session. It was the weekend.

I pressed a button on the security device to the right, a large pad with keys, a speaker, and a screen. There was a click, followed by three rings. I waited, but no answer came. I pressed the button again and again and again.

Finally, Eric's face appeared on the screen. He looked as if he'd gotten a punk haircut. He squinted tiredly at the screen.

"Sunder? What the hell are you doing here." He glanced sideways. "It's twelve twenty-two, and it's fucking Sunday."

"Open the door," I demanded.

"Go back home. I'll see you tomorrow."

"Open the door!"

"No."

He lifted a hand to turn off the device. Anger seethed in my gut. I would not leave until I got the answers I needed.

OPEN THE DOOR! I pushed my wish forward with all my will. My message wasn't made up of words but of need and want and fury.

On the screen, Eric's eyes grew wide.

OPEN THE DOOR! I repeated.

My muscles rippled, the change coming over me. I slammed my arm against the glass door. Pain shot into my shoulder. A crack appeared in the thick glass.

"Shit, Sunder, calm down! Don't ruin my fucking door," Eric growled. "I'll be right there."

The door slid open. I stared at it perplexed, rubbing my arm. I took two deep breaths, heeding Eric's words to calm down. I rolled my shoulders and neck, pushing away my anger.

Settle down, Red. It's all right.

My wolf pulled back, letting me keep control. More and more, as I grew to understand her, she seemed to listen to me. I walked into Eric's house, measuring my steps, trying desperately to temper my fury.

I reached the living room and waited, eyes roving over the many sitting areas and modern art. This section of the house felt nothing like a home. Instead it made me think of an office building, though I suspected that, deep in the bowels of the house, Eric kept a lair much different than this. I had seen a hint of it in his study the day we'd met. The place had been warm and inviting with a massive fireplace and tons of books.

A couple of minutes later, Eric appeared through a door in the back. He wore a pair of blue pajama pants and a gray T-shirt. His bare feet slapped against the polished concrete floor. His brown hair stood on end, and two-day stubble covered his jaw. Piercing blue eyes stared at me, cold and cautious.

"You are part of a bargain I shouldn't have made," he said tiredly. He had agreed to train me to pay a favor he owed to Damien Ward.

"Am I an alpha?" I expected him to laugh in my face, but he only continued staring coldly. "ANSWER ME!" I demanded.

"Ask your wolf, not me. She knows the answer."

I shook my head.

He sighed, scrubbed at his face, and sat on the nearest sofa, a leather number with slick lines and stainless steel framing.

"The two times you've trained with me," he said after a moment, "you've always heeled to my commands, though you fought me every step of the way. I thought you might be a beta, a strong one at that, but now I know I was wrong." He glanced up. "Yes, you're an alpha. I heard your thoughts clear and strong."

I took a step back, the horror of this revelation hitting me full force. "No," I whispered, wishing it weren't true, but knowing deep in my heart that it was.

"No?" Eric asked, puzzled. "In case you don't know, being an alpha is a good thing when you're a werewolf, especially if you're female *and* packless like you are. You should be glad."

His words registered at some level, but all I could do was think of Stephen and Blake. It couldn't be true. Stephen couldn't be responsible for… for what? The rhabo? The unrest in the Skew community? His own kidnapping?

Eric stood and took two steps in my direction. "What's going on, Sunder?"

I stared at my hands while my lungs pumped air in and out as if they were getting paid for overtime. Could I trust Eric with what I'd discovered? At his party, the day I met him, he had been serving rhabo, then that vampire girl had shown up at his door, demanding more of the glittery, deadly liquid. Did that make him a provider? A dealer? Jake thought so. He had warned me to be careful. But I didn't know for sure, so telling him what I knew could turn out to be a huge mistake. Still, there were other things I could discuss with him, things that terrified me.

"I feel I'm changing all the time," I said.

He nodded. "It might take some time for your wolf to settle and reach her full potential."

"I'm afraid I will become a different person, someone I won't recognize."

Eric huffed. "You don't have to find out you're a werewolf for that to happen. You're young, Sunder. You haven't lived enough to know, but there are many things that can alter you. Time doesn't pass in vain."

I sank on the sofa Eric had just vacated. "I don't want any of this. I want to go back to normal."

"Stop whining," he spat, his voice cutting, unsympathetic. "You've nothing to complain about."

His expression had turned hard as if etched in rock. I swallowed the lump in my throat. If I wanted sympathy, I was barking up the wrong tree. I suspected Eric had lost his heart when he'd lost his family.

"You haven't lost anything," he said. "You have instead gained what many others would kill for. You have no idea how many young werewolves would move heaven and earth to have what you have."

"I would give it to them gladly."

"Don't be pathetic." His voice boomed through the large room, startling me.

I slowly rose to my feet. "Stop yelling at me."

To my surprise, he threw his head back and laughed. "Few would dare talk to me like that, and I only allow it because of your ignorance, but let me make it clear now, alpha or not, you will follow my lead if you want our little arrangement to continue."

He stared me down until I looked away. I wanted him to keep teaching me—now more than ever. I needed to know how being an alpha changed things for me. Would it make it easier or harder to remain packless? Did it make a relationship between Jake and me impossible?

At the thought of Jake, I grabbed my head, feeling the world around me falling apart. He was engaged to Allison Blackridge. Their relationship was nothing more than an arranged marriage meant to make the Knight pack stronger. He didn't love her. He loved me. He had said so himself. And yet, he was going along with it, hadn't even had the balls to tell me about it himself.

"You were right," I said. "Jake is getting married."

Eric grunted. "Not this again. I'm not a relationship counselor, so please, spare me."

I didn't care if he didn't want to talk about it. He was supposed to be helping me. "Jake loves me and not that simpering blonde his grandfather is forcing him to marry. I don't have a pack to help them grow their numbers, but could being an alpha make a difference?"

His mouth twisted to one side. "If anything, it makes things worse. I already told you that the Knight pack is old-fashioned. They want their females submissive. As if that weren't enough, alpha and alpha don't always mix when it comes to mating. You can't have two werewolves trying to lead. If you know what's good for you, you'll forget about Jacob Knight and find you a nice weak beta to keep you warm at night." He sighed tiredly. "Look, it's been a long week. Go home, Sunder. Come back tomorrow, and just know that this whole ordeal could be a lot harder for you. Be grateful for the strength you've inherited."

"Inherited?" I echoed, my thoughts racing. "Does… does that mean my father was also an alpha?"

One of his eyes twitched, almost imperceptibly. "Most likely." He made a dismissive gesture with his hand that seemed forced.

"You're hiding something." I didn't know why I was so sure, but Eric knew more than he was letting on.

He didn't deny it. He simply went on staring at me.

"You know who my father is," I said.

He nodded. "Damien told me."

Of course the mage knew. That bastard.

I turned my back on Eric, anger digging its claws into my heart. I struggled to breathe. My chest felt tight as if ready to burst with the well of emotions raging inside of me.

I hadn't wanted to know who my biological father was. It had felt like a betrayal to Dad. But not just that, learning I was a werewolf had been enough of a disruption to my life. The knowledge would've been something else to upset me and distract me, more fuel to an already raging fire.

Did I still feel the same way? Or was I ready to learn who he was?

"He left," my mother had said, which had made me wonder what would have happened if he hadn't. Maybe my parents would have divorced and my youngest sister would've never been born. Maybe I would've grown up in a pack as a werewolf. The idea made my head spin.

"Who is he?" I found myself asking without thinking.

"You have to ask your mother about that. I don't get involved in family dramas."

I still wasn't talking to my mother, so that wasn't an option. "Do I want to know?"

Eric said nothing.

I turned and faced him. "Do I?"

"Leave me out of this, Sunder."

"Is he in St. Louis?"

"Dammit! How do you want me to tell you I don't want to get involved?"

Weirdly, I was suddenly glad that he hadn't answered my questions. *Gah!* I grabbed my head, feeling so confused. I both wanted and didn't want to know, though the latter option seemed to be winning the race.

"I didn't ask for any of this," I said. "I don't want to change, but I feel it in my blood, and I can't stop it. I'm afraid of what I'll become."

Eric's heavy expression lightened a fraction. "You'll be all right," he said, though there wasn't any conviction in his voice.

"You're lying."

He made a gesture toward the door, then turned and walked away. "I have three more sessions with you. Make sure you make the most of them."

He left me standing in the dark room, my anger subdued but still simmering.

Jake was getting married.

Stephen might be the one behind all the unrest in the city.

And I was the daughter of an alpha werewolf whose identity was starting to make me curious.

By the witchlights, at this rate, my life would soon be unrecognizable. Just as I feared.

CHAPTER 2

I drove aimlessly for hours until the sun rose, and I realized I'd better head home before Rosalina woke up and found that I was gone.

She was probably already worried that I had spent all of Saturday in bed. After finding out that Jake was engaged, I'd cried my eyes out on her shoulder, then I'd gone into my bedroom and didn't come out. She let me be, only knocking on my door to ask if I wanted anything for dinner. If I knew her well though, she wouldn't let me wallow in my misery for much longer. And maybe she had taught me well because I had no intention of doing that anyway.

One day crying over Jake was more than enough. I'd promised myself never to cry over a man again, and though I had failed miserably, I'd learned a lot since last time. I knew I had a life to live whether or not he was part of it. No man, not even Jake, was worth giving up for. This had only been a setback, one I could pick myself from without her help. My big girl panties had gotten steel-clad, it seemed.

On the way home, I picked up a box of Rosalina's favorite bagels along with hazelnut cream cheese and hot coffees. Today was supposed to be a happy day. I had the keys to my new condo, and I finally had time to go check it out. Also, my new furniture was arriving this morning, and I had to be there to let the delivery crew in.

It was something simple and normal to do. Nothing like worrying about my friend being the monster we'd been fighting against, or dealing with the knowledge of my ex's engagement, or wondering about my biological father's identity. Besides, I wanted time to digest my alpha status, and the memory of Blake's cry for help. Maybe I was wrong about what I'd heard. Maybe it had really been a nightmare and nothing else.

When I got home, Rosalina was still in bed. I set the table with plates, put the bagels on a tray, and got utensils and our favorite vanilla creamer out of the refrigerator. I didn't have to wait too long before she shuffled out of her bedroom, wearing a mid-thigh, baggy T-shirt and a groggy expression.

Her green eyes opened wide as she saw the spread. "Yum, you were up early. Couldn't sleep?" She scanned my face, her expression sympathetic.

"I slept enough." I forced a smile. I had decided not to tell her what I had found out about myself and Stephen. Not yet, anyway. I wanted our morning to be as normal as possible, without any werewolf drama to taint a moment we'd both been looking forward to.

We sat at the table and started on our breakfast. The cinnamon crunch bagels were my favorite, and I ate two, both with a thick layer of cream cheese on top. My coffee turned a nice caramel color as I poured creamer into it.

Rosalina perused her phone and, after only a minute, set it

down, disgusted. "Vampires are still killing werewolves, blaming them for rhabo."

"I thought the drug bust would help," I said, "but it's like the drug's influx hasn't stopped."

"I know." She sighed. "But never mind that. Are you excited?" Rosalina asked cautiously.

"Damn right I am. I've been waiting for this moment for a very long time."

She scrunched up her face. "I'll hate to see you go. It's been nice having you around."

"Yeah, I've enjoyed staying with you, too, but sooner or later, you would get sick of me. When the howling at the full moon and the werewolf orgies begin, you won't want me here."

"You're kidding, right?"

I twisted my mouth noncommittally.

"O-kay, so when are you moving out?" She made it sound as if it couldn't be fast enough.

"Oh, admit it, the idea of an orgy excites you."

"Ew, nope. I'm a one-man kind of gal."

"Boring," I said in a singsong voice.

She rolled her green eyes, aware that I was joking. I wasn't too far from becoming a nun. I wondered if they accepted werewolves at the convent?

Thirty minutes later, I was pulling my Camaro into my condo complex and scanned the card they'd given me during closing. For a second, I was worried it wouldn't work, but the gate arm lifted out of the way, and we drove into the underground garage.

I parked in the spot marked with the number 216. Some of the giddiness and excitement I'd been expecting pushed past the simmering anger that had made itself comfortable inside my chest, allowing me to enjoy the moment.

We rode the elevator to the second floor, exited into a long carpeted corridor, and walked toward unit 216. I was carrying Cupid's fishbowl and food with me.

"This is it," I said, handing the bowl over to Rosalina.

My hand shook as I keyed the lock. When I threw the door open, the scent of floor polish and fresh paint greeted me. I walked in, my smile growing wider and warmer at the sight of my little condo with its walnut-colored hardwood floors and beige walls. The open floor plan gave the kitchen full view of the dining room and the living room. The cute balcony looked onto the tree-lined street below, and I could already picture myself enjoying my morning coffee there. It wasn't much, but it was mine. Rosalina and I had made it possible with our hard work and vision for our business.

"Home sweet home," Rosalina said, setting Cupid on the kitchen counter, then walking toward the French doors that led to the balcony to draw back the blinds.

Late April sunlight spilled inside, making everything look cheerier, if a little bit too beige. I had plans for bolder colors that suited my personality and would complement the furniture and décor.

For once, the delivery crew was on time, and the bedroom and living room set Rosalina and I had purchased were in place before lunch. We removed the plastic wrap and inspected each piece to make sure there was no damage. Then we positioned everything the way I wanted and took a step back to admire our handiwork.

"It's already taking shape," I said, glad I'd picked the navy sofa set and not the cream one I had been considering. It looked great in the space.

"Looks amazing!" She smiled. "When are we throwing your first rager?" She swayed her hips, pulling some very sexy salsa moves.

"Never." I made the sign of the cross at her. "I don't want my neighbors to hate me."

"I'm so glad you're not letting anything dampen your mood today. How about we celebrate with lunch?"

"I'd love to, but I texted Tom earlier. I haven't had a chance to talk to him in a while."

As much as I would've liked to forget about Stephen and what I'd heard in my nightmare, I hadn't been able to do it, and Blake's voice kept ringing inside my head, calling for Stephen's help.

I had to tell Detective Tom Freeman about it. Of course, he would probably think I was crazy. He still didn't believe that Blake was alive, and that I'd fought him at the Pulse Inc. warehouse—not that I could blame him. Everything had happened so fast that I hadn't had the opportunity to tell him the entire truth about me... that I was a werewolf, which had allowed me to fight Blake's massive wolf and survive.

Rosalina looked a little disappointed.

"Um, what if you come with us?" I added quickly. "I know Tom won't mind, and there's been a… new development."

"You mean besides Jake's engagement?"

I nodded.

"Oh, man! Lately you've been a regular Pandora's box, Triple T."

I puffed my cheeks and blew air out. "A Pandora's box is starting to seem like nothing compared to this mangy werewolf."

Red bristled at the comment. *You're the one with mange, not me.*

Maybe that was true. I only itched when in my human form, never as a werewolf. Actually, when I shifted, everything felt just right, easier. Maybe if I never shifted back and I moved to the Canadian tundra, life would be better.

Damn right it would be, Red piped in.

"I'm up for lunch with Detective Tom Freeman," Rosalina said.

"Great, let's go then."

I fed Cupid a few pellets before leaving. Then we were on our way. As I drove, I wondered if Tom would believe me. I hoped he would. He had the resources to investigate Stephen and find out if he was behind all the chaos that was destroying the peace in the city. I really hoped I could get him on my side.

CHAPTER 3

We met Tom at his favorite steakhouse restaurant. He was dressed in jeans and a forest green polo shirt, looking relaxed as he enjoyed his free day. He looked handsome, like an older version of Idris Elba.

"Ladies," he greeted, "it's so good to see you."

We walked in and were seated within minutes. Several TVs played sports channels. Tom's eyes drifted from a basketball to a football to a hockey game in under a minute. The poor guy was in dude heaven and couldn't handle himself.

I cleared my throat to get his attention. His dark gaze drifted to mine. He shifted in his seat as he noticed my expression, and all at once, his demeanor changed and he became Detective Freeman.

"You're gonna help unravel me, kiddo?" he asked. "'Cause I'm all tied up in knots with what's been going on lately. I can tell something's going on with you. That business at the warehouse… I still have a ton of questions."

"There's definitely something going on with me." I smiled sadly. "And I hope that what I'm about to tell you will help undo some of those gnarly knots."

As quickly and succinctly as I could, I told Tom everything, from finding out I was a werewolf up to my fight with Blake. He listened, opening and closing his mouth several times as if to say something, but never interrupting. When I was done explaining, I stopped to glance around to see if anyone around us had tuned in to our conversation, but I shouldn't have worried. Everyone was distracted with their food, their lunch companions, or the big-screen TVs.

"A werewolf?" Tom said once he regained his voice. He blinked several times as if his internal processor was overheated. Maybe I had short-circuited the poor guy. He scrubbed his goatee, then his head. His T-bone steak sat forgotten in front of him, growing cold.

Rosalina attacked a huge onion ring and gave the detective a sympathetic nod. "Crazy, huh?"

"What do you think now, Tom?" I asked after a moment of silence. "Does that help you believe that Blake is alive? Or does it make it harder?"

"It certainly explains…" he started slowly, his mind ramping back up to speed, "the state of your clothes when we got to the warehouse. It also makes it more likely that you could've defeated a strong beta like Blake—if that was indeed Blake."

"So you still don't believe I fought him," I said.

He shrugged. "I think *you* think you did, but maybe some of that rhabo got you…" He twirled a finger over his temple.

Maybe I should have been mad that he didn't believe me, but I wasn't. The detective was all about the facts, things that added up like equations.

"There's something else," I said. "Something new." I turned to Rosalina with a pointed look that let her know this would also be new to her.

She set her fork down and pushed the plate away. "I'm ready… I think."

The fearful tone in her voice made my heart tighten. How much more would she be able to take? When she joined me in a partnership for our agency, she didn't sign up for any of this. At this rate, one day, she would decide I wasn't worth the trouble, and our agency, which we'd worked so hard to build, would go up in flames.

But what else could I do? I had to tell her, then hope that this alpha business wasn't going to cause more disruptions than we already had.

"I think I know who's behind the rhabo influx into the city," I said.

"Is that so?" Tom rested his elbows on the table and leaned forward, his expression more skeptical than ever. He was probably remembering how we'd sent him after Damien Ward with claims that the mage had rhabo in his house. The detective had gotten a warrant and found nothing in Damien's home. No wonder his trust was broken.

"I may be wrong," I said. "My skills as a werewolf are only beginning to manifest, and I'm only starting to understand what I am and how everything works. You see, I didn't learn this until last night, but I'm an alpha."

"Holy witchlights!" Rosalina exclaimed, pressing a hand to her mouth. "How do you know that?"

"Alphas are able to push their thoughts into other werewolves' minds. They are also able to listen to their thoughts when *they* project them out."

"Shit," Rosalina said in a whisper.

"This particular skill didn't come to the surface right away," I continued. "But last night, I understood something that happened at the warehouse that I didn't fully grasp in the beginning. The memory came back to me in a sort of… dream state." I would have rather not mention this part—Tom would probably think I was cuckoo-bananas—but since I wasn't a hundred percent sure about what I'd experienced, I felt it was better to be honest.

"A dream state?" Tom repeated, a deep frown line appearing on his forehead.

Yep, he thought I was five cans short of a six-pack. I shrugged. "It is what it is. I still have to tell you in case what I think I heard is right."

He sighed. "Shoot then."

"While Blake was lying on the floor in pain from the wolfsbane, probably thinking he was going to die, I heard him call out for help inside his mind. At the time, I only felt this awful pressure in my temples, but last night, my subconscious was able to interpret the message he was sending out."

"Oh, my God," Rosalina said. "I'm on pins and needles. What did he say?"

"He called out for Stephen Erickson's help."

"What?!" Rosalina asked in a breathy voice.

"Stephen might have been there in the warehouse," I added. "He might have been the one that helped Blake attack Jake and the one who helped Blake get away."

I waited for Tom to say something, but he just sat there, his dark eyes roving over all the items on the table.

"I want to be wrong," I said. "I don't want it to be him."

Tom still said nothing.

"I'm mad as a hatter, right? I keep thinking Jake would have recognized Stephen. He must know his wolf. They're friends. Unless Stephen did something to disguise his wolf at the warehouse, which is entirely possible with a mage helping him."

Tom pulled out his wallet, fished out several twenty dollar bills, and set them on the table. "This should cover the check and tip." He pushed his chair back, getting ready to leave.

"Where are you going?" I asked.

"To the station. I need to go over the case files with this new perspective in mind."

"Why? Is there something…?" I didn't know what to ask, so I let the question hang.

"There are a few things that don't add up about Stephen's kidnapping," he said. "I can't discuss details, but this may shed new light on the case. I should go now. If you learn anything else, don't hesitate to let me know."

I nodded and watched him leave, feeling my heart sink like lead.

"If… Stephen faked his own kidnapping," Rosalina started tentatively, "does that mean he sent those people to kidnap you?"

Tears pooled in my eyes as I played with my napkin, my entire being shrinking away from that idea.

"I guess," I said after a few beats. I almost choked on the words. I had risked my life for him, had fought a huge shifter and two vampires, faced Bernadetta Fiore, had even killed someone because I thought he was in danger. All for what? A fake kidnapping?

"Why would he do that?"

This was an important question that in my confused state of mind I had barely considered. Rosalina and I exchanged a glance, both frowning as we thought about the possibilities.

"He knew I would try to find him," I said, thinking out loud. "So maybe he wanted to make sure I didn't ruin his plans, but why not just kill me?"

"Because he likes you," she said.

I frowned and shook my head.

"He does. But why fake his kidnapping in the first place?"

"Maybe he did it to get rid of his father?" I said, thinking back at how mad Stephen had always seemed toward Ulfen.

"Yeah," she agreed. "And it worked. Ulfen is in jail now and accused of kidnapping and attempted murder, too."

That would mean that Stephen had also sent that mage, Jenson Boyle, to fake an attack at the pizzeria. I nodded slowly as several pieces seemed to fall into place.

When I had talked to Ulfen about tracking Stephen, he had seemed genuinely concerned. And after we found him, Ulfen had been relieved, glad that nothing had happened to his son and heir. It hadn't been a sham.

"If he did kidnap himself, he would've had to cut his own finger off," Rosalina said, cringing.

I shivered at the thought. It would take a truly cold and deranged man to do that, and that was not the Stephen I knew. He was lighthearted, gentle, and carefree. Whoever was behind the cunning scheme, causing unrest in the city would have to be greedy and power hungry, two qualities Ulfen had been trying to instill in his son but that Stephen had adamantly resisted. Or at least, that was the way it had always seemed.

"It makes no sense." I shook my head.

"Are you going to tell Jake?"

"I don't know."

That was another thing I had tried not to think about. I didn't want to see Jake—not ever again. But he needed to know that the man he thought of as his friend and who he'd moved heaven and earth to help was not who he thought.

We sat quietly for several minutes while the waiter removed our barely-touched food.

"Well," Rosalina said after a long moment, "if you think about it, there isn't much we can do. It's not really our problem to solve. This is something for the police to take care of. Wouldn't you say?"

I nodded, letting her words sink in. I'd been so immersed in this entire situation that I felt like I was part of it, that there must be something I could do to fix it, but this was much bigger than me. The world had been revolving at this same messed up pace before I got caught in its dizzying dance. There was no reason why I couldn't leave the party for much slower pastures.

"Yes, you're right," I agreed.

"Good, now all you have to do is focus on wolf training for a few more sessions with Eric and on our customers, which brings me to Aaron and Josh."

I winced. I was still feeling terrible about leading Aaron to Josh, a vampire with a death sentence hanging around his neck like a noose. I couldn't keep the money Aaron had paid for our services when all I'd done was invite misery into his life. If Josh died, Aaron would be devastated for the rest of his life, and finding happiness with anyone else would be nearly impossible now that he'd experienced love with his true mate.

If I had known that Josh was sick, I would have never introduced them to each other. It would have been unethical and not to mention cruel.

"What are we gonna do about them?" Rosalina asked. "We have to decide something."

"I know but how do you break the news to them?"

"Maybe before we do anything," Rosalina started, looking chagrined, "we should talk to Damien. He might know of a way to help Josh. He's clearly involved in all of this, trying to fight the good fight."

I frowned. "I don't think that's a good idea, Rosalina. I don't trust him."

"He said he wanted to stop Blake."

"He was hiding something. Couldn't you tell?"

She shrugged, looking noncommittal.

"You like him too much. I think you can't be objective when it comes to Damien Ward."

"I don't think he's a bad guy, Toni. I have a good feeling about him."

"And I have a bad one. He kept me under a spell for twenty years, who does that?"

She leaned back on her chair and cautiously said, "He did it to help your mother."

"Two wrongs don't make a right. They both screwed with me. I may never be the same. You have no idea how confused I feel, how hard it is to process all of these changes."

She reached across the table and laid her hand on top of mine. "I do know it's hard. I pay attention, and I'm trying to help. But we need to do something about Aaron and Josh, so maybe I can go see Damien and talk to him."

"No way." I shook my head. "We sent the cops after him, and he's mad at us, remember?"

"Do you have any other ideas to help Aaron and Josh? Because I would rather go to them with help than with the news that their relationship was doomed before it even started."

Once more, she was right. We had to do everything in our power to help the couple. We owed it to them.

"Okay," I said with a sigh, "let's go see Damien."

CHAPTER 4

As we made our way downtown toward Damien's house, we drove the Camaro with the top down, playing a pop station on the radio. Rosalina was humming and moving her head to the beat of the song. Her good mood was infectious, and soon we were both singing and pumping our fists in the air.

The light feeling that possessed me was welcomed, and it made me miss how things had been just a few weeks ago before Jake made it back into my life. It was amazing how one person could screw up someone's life, from zero to hell.

We parked across from Damien's crumbling, goth house and crossed the street. I was about to ring the bell when I noticed the door was cracked open. Rosalina and I exchanged a glance of concern. I rang the bell anyway and waited. There was no response. I knocked next and poked my head in.

"Hello, anybody home? Damien?"

No answer still.

We walked further into the foyer, leaving the door open a crack, the way it had been. The place was eerily silent. I glanced toward the landing at the top of the marble staircase, admired the modern interior, and elegant décor, but saw no signs of the mage. We headed slowly toward the kitchen, the only place in the house we'd visited. We were halfway there when there was a loud crash somewhere in the house.

I stopped abruptly, putting a hand out to stop Rosalina. "I think we should get out of here and call the police."

She nodded, and we started to backtrack the way we'd come when two figures appeared in front of the exit. One was a black wolf, and the other a man. I recognized both of them immediately.

Blake Foster and Jenson Boyle.

The wolf was as massive as I remembered, his head reaching past Jenson's elbow, his shoulders heaving with anger. His eyes shone yellow as he fixed them on me. The mage was dressed all in black and wore the same leather cloak I'd seen on him before. His bright red hair stood on end as usual, but unlike the last time we'd met, his eyes shone copper, not blue, which meant he'd powered up his magic to the next level. Not good.

I stepped in front of Rosalina. Red stirred, itching to come out, but I held her back as my mind sped, trying to figure out a way out. If I shifted, it would mean a certain fight, one I couldn't win, not without wolfsbane bullets or magic of some kind.

"You're trespassing," I said, my voice sounding steadier than I felt.

"Hello, little tracker," the mage said. "Fancy meeting you here."

The wolf growled in turn.

"Where's Damien?" Rosalina's voice trembled with emotion, revealing her fear. She thought they had hurt him.

"Unfortunately," Jenson said, "he's not here. I wanted us to have a tête-à-tête, see how we measure up now that I've earned my copper wings." He gestured toward his eyes.

Rosalina let out a shaky breath of relief.

"But enough talking," the mage said as the wolf stepped forward, lowering his head and growling deep in his chest. "I think both Blake and I have a score to settle with you, little tracker. You've been slippery, but what do you know? You've come to find us."

"Run!" I said, turning then pushing Rosalina toward the kitchen.

I didn't have to tell her twice. She ran full pelt with me on her heels. The wolf's sharp claws clicked against the polished floor as it tried to gain traction. At the kitchen's entrance, we veered right. A stream of magic *whooshed* behind me, narrowly missing me as I turned. The attack flew wide and hit the shelves on the opposite wall, blowing Damien's espresso machine into millions of little pieces.

"Find a way out," I urged Rosalina as I invited Red to the fight.

The shift happened in the blink of an eye. My clothes ripped into hundreds of tatters, flying across the kitchen and landing on top of the island and floor. I turned to face our attackers as Rosalina exited through a door in the far corner.

I willed her to run faster and find the final door that would lead her out of here. In the meantime, I planned to give her all the time she needed to get to safety.

I let out an ear-piercing growl and stood my ground.

Jenson and Blake came around the corner and skidded to a stop when they saw me.

"You were right," the mage said, "the little tracker is a werewolf. What a surprise."

Blake shook his big head in challenge. He looked pissed, really pissed, and he wanted payback. I had bested him and put him through a lot of pain, now he wanted to do the same to me.

Words to taunt him entered my mind, and I almost pushed them forward using my alpha powers, but something told me to stop, not to reveal what I was. Maybe there would be more I could learn, if he didn't know I could hear his thoughts. Red fought against my reasoning, wishing to express her dominance, but she quickly caught my drift and, to my surprise, went along with it. More and more, it seemed our thoughts and feelings were not opposed and we were reaching an understanding.

Nice. I can get used to this, Red.

The mage huffed as the black wolf advanced. "Okay, she's all yours, but you owe me."

Blake leaped toward me, teeth bared, eyes blazing with hatred.

I jumped out of the way and ran around the island. Blake landed on the smooth floor, skidded along, and crashed against the wall. Pushing with my hind legs, I took two bounding leaps toward the mage. His eyes shot wide open as I flew in his direction. He staggered backward, his hands and fingers twisting in rapid patterns as he prepared a spell. Before he could manage, my front paws hit his chest. The crackle of magic surged in his fingers. He fell backward but managed to wrap his hands around my front legs. A shock of electrifying magic zapped through every nerve in my body. I yelped, feeling as if I were on fire.

We fell in a heap. I tumbled away, whining in pain. I tried to stand but fell back down. My limbs twitched as if bolts of electricity were shooting through them.

Get up, Red. Get up!

I clenched my teeth, and growling with effort, fought through the pain, and stood. Blake barreled into me, his huge maw snapping and closing around my ear as I attempted to get out of the way. He bit into the tender skin. Gritting my teeth, I turned my head to one side. My ear tore in half, but I was free. Blood slid down the side of my face.

Rage bloomed in my chest. I went for Blake's neck, but he was too fast, and my teeth snapped shut around empty air. He came at me again. I dodged out of the way, able to move faster since I was smaller.

I whirled and ran toward the foyer, headed for the door, but it slammed shut of its own accord. I turned sharply and dashed toward the grand staircase. I took the steps four and five at a time. Blake followed close behind, bounding, swatting at my back legs, trying to trip me. On the landing, a table with a marble top and ornate legs held a large vase. I jumped on top of it and swiped the vase with one paw, aiming for Blake. He tried to duck out of the way, but the vase crashed against his front legs, sending him sprawling.

As he fell, I hopped on top of him and bit into the scruff of his neck, tasting blood, and dialing my instincts to frenzy levels. He bucked, trying to throw me off, but I held on, my jaw clamped tightly around fur and flesh.

He bounded down the steps and ran at the railing, crushing me between his large body and a marble column. Bones snapped in my back and fresh, vicious pain flashed through me, nearly blinding me. My jaw came loose, and I fell limp onto the steps. Blake shook himself, splattering blood all around, then came at me, with murder in his eyes.

I shrank as if that could get me away from his vicious teeth. I sensed his delight at seeing me broken, helpless. He thirsted for blood, got pleasure from inflicting pain. I tried to stand, to fight, but I collapsed.

Blake licked his lips and pounced.

Then he froze in midair, his maw wide open, dripping saliva.

His eyes flashed yellow as he blinked in surprise. His body started floating toward the ceiling, going higher and higher.

"Blake Foster," Damien's delighted voice echoed through the large space, "I have been looking for you."

The black wolf snarled, his forelegs dancing, scratching helplessly at the air as he rose and rose.

Strolling casually, Damien appeared in my field of vision. He wore a top hat and a cloak with red lining. His white hair clashed with the youthfulness of his features.

"Toni, is that you, love?" he asked.

I whimpered in answer, willing my body to heal, to knit itself together, but my healing abilities weren't as fast as I would've liked. Would I even be able to recover from this? For all I knew I would be in traction for months, lying on a bed with a pooping hole in the middle of the mattress.

"What to do with you?" Damien said in a contemplative voice as he looked up at the dangling wolf. "I wonder how many bones you would break if I drop you from that height. It wouldn't kill you, but it would hurt like hell."

"Put him down," Jenson snarled from the side.

Damien shifted his shoulders slightly and glanced to his left. Jenson inched into my line of vision, holding Rosalina close to his body, one hand around her throat and the other one crackling with magic right next to her head.

Oh, no!

"Put him down, I said, unless you want me to fry your friend's brain."

Damien scanned Rosalina from head to toe, an expression of cool indifference shaping his features. "Go right ahead," he said. "I barely know her."

The bastard! How could he?

I let out a bark of protest and tried to stand, but I was too broken to do anything.

Jenson moved his hand closer to Rosalina's head, murderous intent in his copper-tinted eyes. He wasn't bluffing. And, either way, he wouldn't care if my best friend died.

I hooked my claws around the edge of one of the marble steps, attempting to move, fighting to reach her. I had to do something, anything. I couldn't lose her. If anything happened to Rosalina…

Jenson's magic crackled, brushing her hair.

"All right, all right, I'll put him down," Damien said between clenched teeth.

I deflated with relief, my body going limp.

Damien lowered his arms slowly, bringing Blake down. He set him on the floor, not-too-gently, though he kept him under his control, frozen in place.

"You first," Damien said.

"No, you, Ward."

Damien's right eye twitched. "At the same time, then."

Jenson shrugged as if it were all the same to him. "On the count of three. One." He pushed Rosalina forward, but he kept his hands at the ready.

Damien flicked his wrist, and Blake slid forward as if on skates.

"Two," Jenson said, lowering one crackling hand.

At the same time, Damien gave Blake another push forward.

"Three."

Rosalina staggered into Damien's arms, crossing paths with Blake, who rushed to Jenson's side and whirled around, threateningly.

"Now get the fuck out of my house," Damien snarled as he stepped protectively in front of Rosalina and raised his hands toward the home invaders.

Jenson crouched and raised his hands, too. Blake lowered his head and growled.

"If I were you," Damien said, a crooked smirk tipping his lips. "I would run." His gaze flicked to me for a moment, full of concern and caution for only an instant, then he continued. "You're too green, Jenson. When did you become a Copper Mage? Yesterday? Very unwise to try to test your newly acquired powers against someone like me. I know things you can only dream of." Flames appeared at the tips of his fingers, growing long and short, dancing in a tantalizing way. "I don't want to fight. I like my home very much and would rather avoid the destruction, but if you push it, I will turn you into a lump of charcoal."

Jenson licked his lips and closed his hands into fists to hide their slight trembling. Next to him, Blake bared his teeth and growled, ready for any amount of destruction.

"Let's go, Blake. We've done what we came to do," Jenson said, smiling with glee.

The wolf raked his claws over the hardwood floor, gouging deep grooves in its surface as they retreated toward the front door.

"This isn't over, Ward," Jenson said, then they turned tail and ran.

Damien stood silent for a few beats. At last, he stomped toward the door, cursing. He slammed it shut, laid his hands on it, and muttered something under his breath.

"That cocky rooster shouldn't have been able to get through my protective spells." He paced along the door, tapping his temple, then faced it again and muttered something else as he sent another spell from his fingers. The magic hit the door at its center and spread outward, glowing and crackling, reaching toward the rest of the house, its tendrils crawling over the walls and floors until it sealed with a pop in the center of the ceiling.

When he was done, he turned to face us, his copper eyes assessing the situation. He pointed at Rosalina. "You all right?"

She was hugging herself, sweat plastering black hair to her cheeks, fear and shock giving her features a wild edge.

"I'm fine," she said, her voice firm. "Help Toni."

Damien nodded once and walked in my direction, his leather shoes tapping against the floor. He knelt next to me and put a hand on top of my head. He closed his eyes, letting his fingers trail down my spine. Tingling heat met my skin wherever he touched. The pain slowly dimmed to a dull ache, and I felt my broken bones align to their correct positions, and my ear knit itself.

I exhaled, my body settling with abandon on the cold marble steps.

Damien removed his cloak and draped it over me. It was incredibly warm like the heated blanket Nonna used during cold New York winters.

"Shift," the mage said. "It'll speed up the healing process if you go back and forth a few times."

I did as I was told. The first shift was painful and awkward, seeming to happen in stages and leaving me with a tail sticking out of my bottom for far longer than it was comfortable. The next couple of shifts were smoother, happening seconds apart from each other. Then the pain was gone, and I felt right as rain.

Clutching the cloak close to my body, I got to my feet, amazed at how great I felt, especially considering that death had seemed like a distinct possibility just moments ago. The idea of that bed with a hole in the middle had seemed very real for a moment, but thank God for mages and amazing healing skills.

Damien scanned me up and down as if to make sure his work was done, then he rushed down the steps and through the corridor to the right of the staircase. There was an edge of panic in his movements, a sort of desperation and tired resignation.

Rosalina and I exchanged a curious glance, then went after him. We found him in an ample workroom that looked a lot like my potions alcove except on a grander scale. There were several worktables and a large armoire with carved doors and metal handles, their surfaces littered with glassware: pipettes, beakers, tubes, and funnels.

The mage stood in front of a large table, his hands splayed on its top, his head lowered in defeat. A mixture of strong scents rode the air and hit me as soon as I walked in. Broken glass peppered the floor, its contents scattered and trampled. A couple of tables were tipped over, sticky liquid slowly spreading into large puddles beneath them.

I held my breath as a sharp scent seemed to pierce my nostrils like long needles. Rosalina coughed and pressed a hand over her nose and mouth.

"Bastards," Damien said. "Bastards!" He whirled and faced us, his blotchy pupils large and bottomless.

Was he referring to us? I glanced warily in Rosalina's direction. Was he going to take his anger out on us?

"Uh, when we got here, the door was open," I said in one quick breath to make sure he understood what had happened here. "We have nothing to do with this destruction."

"I know that." He looked at me as if I were stupid. "The house told me everything as I walked in."

Huh? His house talks to him? Um, cool.

He glowered at me. "Still, in a way, it is your fault."

"Our fault?!" Rosalina exclaimed.

"Yes." The mage stared directly at me with his strange copper eyes and blotchy pupils. "You knew where to find Blake, and you lied to me. He got away because you allowed it. He would have never been here today if you had let me go after him."

"I'm sorry," I said. "But can you blame me for not trusting you?" At least now I knew the mage was an enemy of *my* enemies.

"*Dammit!* And I was so close," he said. "I had almost created a cure against rhabo's effects."

CHAPTER 5

Rosalina and I gasped in unison.

"You mean… you mean you were working on a cure, and they destroyed it?" I asked, my heart sinking.

Damien took off his top hat, set in on the worktable, and ran a hand through his short white hair, looking at a loss.

"Can't you start over?" Rosalina asked when he didn't answer my question.

He scoffed. "One of the ingredients I need is nearly impossible to come by." He scrubbed at his face. "I suppose I'm paying for my own mistakes."

Huh? What did he mean by that?

The mage shook his head, then walked out of the room, leaving us behind. He looked utterly defeated and deeply sad, which was odd.

We tiptoed after him.

"You have to keep trying," I urged.

He ignored me, walked past an arched walkway to the right of the workroom, and entered a small sitting area. There, he collapsed on a sofa, looking disgusted.

"You can't give up," I said.

He dragged his copper gaze in my direction. "What is it to you, anyway? Don't werewolves like it when vampires die?" His voice was charged with resentment as he said this.

I bristled. "Hey, that's not fair. You know better. I wasn't raised that way. I think every life has value and should be respected."

He snorted. "So altruistic. Try to remember that when you send the cops to someone's house without any evidence."

Ouch, that hurt. Judging by Rosalina's wince, the comment had also gotten to her.

She stepped forward, holding her chin high. "I'm greatly sorry for that mistake, Damien. I hope you will forgive me."

He raised a white eyebrow and shrugged one shoulder, seemingly accepting her apology, though not in a very gracious way.

Damien waved his hand in the air. "It doesn't matter. I have more important things to worry about. Now, if you don't mind, I would appreciate it if you see yourselves out."

"Let us help you," Rosalina blurted out.

Huh? How did she think we could manage that?

Damien blew air through his nose, and his expression seemed to say we would be as useful to him as two toddlers on a rampage.

"Um, we can help you find the ingredients," she said, clearly grasping at straws.

If she was thinking we could get the ingredients from Elf-hame, she was deluding herself. Damien surely had better access to the Fae realm than we possibly could. He had been a mage for who knew how long and must have contacts we couldn't begin to imagine.

"Look," Damien said, heaving a sigh as if to draw patience from the air, "I don't have time to waste with the likes of you."

"Hey!" I exclaimed. "Don't be an asshat. She's trying to be nice."

"It's all right, Toni." Rosalina smiled sadly. "I guess the best thing we can do is leave and be glad of it. Who wants to deal with a recalcitrant, embittered jerk, anyhow?"

She whirled on her heel and started walking out.

I did the same, and just as we exited the sitting room, I spoke casually to Rosalina. "I thought he might like to know who Blake and Jenson work for, but why waste *our* time with an old man."

Rosalina came to an abrupt stop in front of me. I crashed into her and grabbed onto her shoulders as I stumbled forward and quickly closed the cloak around my body. Damien had appeared in front of her and was blocking the exit.

"Who are you calling an old man?" he demanded with an indignant expression.

I stepped next to Rosalina. "You went to college with my mother, so you are *at least* fifty years old."

"I'll have you know I'm not a day older than you." The few subtle wrinkles he had around his mouth and eyes suddenly smoothed over, making him look a lot younger than me.

I blinked in surprise but recovered quickly. "You may not *look* old, Damien Ward, but you have the heart and the mood of a crotchety sourpuss great great grandfather."

Rosalina put a hand over her mouth and stifled a laugh.

Damien narrowed his eyes and pursed his lips, glaring at us as if he were considering turning us into bird droppings.

I grabbed Rosalina's arm. "C'mon, we'd better go."

The mage put on a smile that made him look like a grimacing monkey—a handsome one, but still. "What was that about telling me who Blake and Jenson work for?"

I shrugged nonchalantly, pulled Rosalina toward the door, and attempted to turn the knob. It didn't budge.

"Open sesame," I said, knocking on the door three times. It still didn't open. I glared at Damien and struck a careful pose, working around the limitations of the cloak. "Let us go."

He crossed his arms in response.

I rolled my eyes. "Ulfen Erickson. They work for Ulfen Erickson. Now, open the door."

"I know Ulfen is not involved," the mage said, "and I have a feeling you know that, too."

Bobbing my head from side to side, I said, "Maybe, but I'm not telling you, *grandpa*."

Damien's face grew red, and a muscle jumped in his jaw. Again, he breathed patience from the air and said, "I'm willing to negotiate for whatever information you possess."

Rosalina and I smiled at each other. Her green eyes glinted, and her mouth stretched into a tiny smile that made her look like the cat that ate the mouse, which was exactly how I felt.

"We want in on this cure thing," Rosalina said.

Damien scrutinized us for a long moment, then asked, "Why?"

"We know someone who needs it," I said.

"I see." He paced from one end of the foyer to the next, considering. "You saw my potions room, it's a disaster. I would have to start from zero, and I may not be able to create a viable cure, and if I do, I may not even be able to create more than one dose."

"One dose?!" I exclaimed. "But there must be thousands of vampires who need it."

"It's far easier to come up with something that destroys than something that creates or restores life. I've been looking into this for some time, and I don't think it's possible to save everyone. Mainly because the ingredients for a cure are rare. Sadly, many vampires have already died, and for most, it's already too late."

"So why try at all?" As soon as the question crossed my lips a possible reason for his interest in a cure came to me.

Damien pressed his lips together into a thin line, unwilling to offer an answer.

"There's someone you want to save," Rosalina said, stealing the words from my mouth.

The mage stopped pacing and stared at the floor. He didn't deny or confirm the assertion, but the pain that etched his face gave us the answer.

"I'm sorry," Rosalina said.

Damien shrugged dismissively as if it didn't matter, but it was clear it did. A lot. I wondered who he knew that needed saving.

"We'd like to help," I said, my conviction building even though I had no clue what we could do. "And we understand what you're saying about the possibility of having only one dose in the end, but I think we'd rather have some hope." I searched Rosalina's gaze. She nodded in agreement.

The mage shook his head. "No. I'm sorry, but I won't help you build pipe dreams. Getting more ingredients is impossible. Now, are you going to tell me who you think is behind all of this? Or do I have to use a truth spell?"

It was a shitty deal, but we figured we owed him after sending the cops after him, so even though the exchange didn't seem quite fair, we told him about Stephen.

CHAPTER 6

The next day, something Damien had said when he found his potential cure destroyed still bothered me. *"I suppose I'm paying for my own mistakes."*

I'd tried not to read too much into it, but the statement kept coming back again and again, and it got tangled with something else that still bugged me, even after many days since my first discovery of rhabo. It was this: as much as Eric seemed opposed to the drug, he had served it as his party. Why?

The insistent subject of their involvement echoed in my head as I stood in front of Eric in his mirrored training room. It was 4 AM, and I'd had to claw myself out of bed to get here, but I'd made it.

I dropped my duffel bag on the floor, lost in thought.

"Chop, chop, Sunder. We don't have all day," Eric urged.

I glanced up, my eyes narrowed.

"Something the matter?" he asked.

I tried to dismiss my nagging questions, but they wouldn't go away. I gave in. "As a matter of fact, yes. I've been wondering… why did you serve rhabo at your party?"

Eric's expression hardened. "Is that how you want to use your limited time with me?"

I shrugged.

He sighed, his shoulders slumping. "Have you wondered why I would throw a party at all?"

It *had* occurred to me. The man was a grump. He wouldn't know "partying" if it nipped him in the balls. He would probably think it was fleas.

"It was extortion," he said. "Parties where rhabo is available to vamps have been going on in the city for some time. It is how they introduced the drug so quickly in the first place. One free dose and the vamps are hooked for life—or maybe I should say 'til true death."

"Extortion?" I said slowly. "That means they have something on you."

He cocked an eyebrow. "Your intellect shines even as early as 4 AM."

My obvious remark had just been my way of asking "what" they had on him—not that I thought he would offer an answer. To my surprise, however, he did.

"Rhabo is my fault," he said.

Huh?

"Damien created it because I asked him to." Eric's expression remained cold. "Its creation was the favor I owed him, which you're helping me repay."

I shook my head, unable to comprehend. "You… Damien… Why?"

"It was meant to kill one vampire, and one vampire only. And it did, but the knowledge of its existence leaked, and someone was able to recreate it. I don't know who yet, but when I find out," his left eye twitched, "I will kill him."

Shivers broke over my arms. I rubbed them absentmindedly. I wondered what vampire he'd killed with the drug. Whoever it had been, they must have been powerful for Eric to need a weapon other than his teeth and claws. Jake had been right. Damien and Eric had everything to do with rhabo.

Eric held my gaze across the room, unflinching, as if daring me to challenge him. He was to blame, even if indirectly, for all the vampires that were dying. The count was in the papers every day, and it kept increasing exponentially.

Yet, that hadn't been his intent. There was someone else behind it all.

"I'm sorry that happened," I said.

He blinked. "You won't condemn me?"

Despite his lack of civility and shitty reputation, Eric didn't strike me as a bad man, only as someone who had suffered much.

He grunted, then asked, "Shall we begin then?"

I nodded. "Yes, lets."

Eric opened his mouth to instruct me, but I spoke first.

"I want to learn to fight," I said.

He raised his eyebrows. "I'm not sure that is the best way to utilize our limited time. You already wasted a good bit of it as it is."

"I've almost been killed twice while trying to defend myself from a bigger wolf, so I think it is."

"Is that so?"

I kicked off my shoes, removed my T-shirt, and threw it on top of my duffel bag. I stood in my sports bra and sweats.

"Give me some pointers." I shook my arms and feet, trying to get limber. I'd learned how to throw good punches in my kick-boxing class, and how to use tricky holds and twists to get free from attackers, but none of that applied to fighting in wolf shape when I didn't have opposable thumbs.

"If you don't mind me asking, who did you fight?" Eric crossed his arms, clearly not in a hurry to teach me about lupine butt-kicking.

I sighed. "His name is Blake Foster."

Eric's eyebrows rose another inch, almost disappearing into his hairline.

"I take it you know him," I said.

"You fought Blake Foster, twice, and lived to tell the tale? I think that means your fighting skills aren't bad at all."

"You're kidding, right? He almost killed me, almost crushed me to death."

"Still, here you are."

I glanced over at the clock on the wall. "Now who's wasting the precious three hours I have with you?"

It was 4:10 AM, and he would kick me out at 7 sharp. I had no more time to stand here talking. Besides, tomorrow and Wednesday were my last two days with him. He and Damien had agreed that Eric would teach me for five days, then I was on my own.

I wasn't ready for that—not by a long shot.

"Precious time, indeed," he said. "Okay, I'll teach you what I can, but I'm not joking when I say that surviving Blake Foster is proof that you have innate fighting skills. Good werewolf hunters, werewolf warriors, werewolf leaders come by their abilities through their blood. There are things that cannot be taught. When humans are born, they are entirely helpless. We're different. We can shift and walk in our wolf shapes right away. We know how to stalk, how to identify the smell of fear and blood, how to tell pack from foe. Your abilities are not trifling. They can be honed, yes, but you are, without a doubt, your father's daughter."

Anger flared in my gut, unbidden. I clenched my fists and took a deep breath, trying to focus on everything else he'd said, not that last bit. I failed.

"For someone who doesn't want to tell me who my father is," I said, "you certainly bring him up enough." I didn't know why I was goading him when I still hadn't made up my mind about whether or not I wanted to know who he was.

"I will not avoid the topic if it's relevant, only because it bothers you. As I was saying, your skills, though still not fully manifested, are considerable. So, let's talk about fighting…" Eric put his hands behind his back and regarded me with his cold blue stare. "The first thing to know, as an alpha, is that fights can be avoided."

"What do you mean?"

"You are a born leader, Sunder, and learning to wield your alpha powers can make others submit to you."

"I don't see how a wolf as big as Blake would submit to me."

Eric smiled with little amusement. "Well, with that attitude…"

"You're serious? I could have made Blake submit?"

"Yes."

Holy shit.

"In theory," he added, bursting my bubble.

I rolled my eyes. Way to get a girl excited.

"Blake is a strong beta," he continued, "and yes, he's big. That's where he gets most of his confidence, but think about this, he belongs to," Eric twirled his hand as if to call words from the aether, "Erickson's pack, right?"

I nodded. He was probably thinking Ulfen and not Stephen, but that didn't make a difference at the moment.

He paced in front of the mirrored wall. "I know for a fact that Erickson's wolf isn't bigger than Blake's, the man's a beast. There are actually very few that can reach that size. Perhaps your Jake could match him in size. I've never seen his wolf, but I've heard rumors that he is impressive."

"Don't make fun of me," I growled, my voice a quiet rumble that I barely recognized. His words had acted like a poker to my anger, stoking it, raising its heat level. "He's not *my* Jake, and he never will be."

"Anger can be a good thing, Sunder, but it can also destroy you."

"I guess you would know."

Eric was on me in an instant, pushing me against the wall, his muscles taut, his fingers stiff at my throat. "You like crossing the line, and you do it recklessly. You might be an alpha, but you're nothing but a little pup compared to me. If you keep pushing your luck, you will regret it."

His blue eyes glowed as he spoke, and his body seemed to pulse with energy like a giant heart. I struggled to get free as my body began to tingle with restless energy, Red itching to be set free.

Heel, Eric's voice boomed inside my head.

The command zapped through my veins like a quick jolt of electricity traversing a copper wire. Every cell in my body seemed to shrink, ready to do as he commanded, as if they didn't belong to me, as if I was only an extension of Eric Cross, another limb that he could flex to his will.

But I wasn't part of him.

I didn't belong to anyone but myself.

A small voice of reason in my head seemed to disagree.

He'll rip your throat out. Just do as he says.

But a bigger and stronger part of me had no intention of giving in.

I'd rather die than submit to him, Red spat.

At once, my will joined hers, dark and wild, and just like that, we were in agreement yet again.

"Get your hands off me," I snarled, my voice so deep and low that it almost matched Eric's. It reverberated through the room, carrying as much command as his.

The grip around my throat slacked infinitesimally, but it was enough. Aware of nothing but my anger and instincts, I grabbed his arm and jerked it away. His claws scratched my throat as his hand came loose. The pain was fuel to my fury, and in one fluid motion, my body went through the shift, releasing my wolf the way the sky releases thunder.

Before I was done, he'd shifted, too. Dropping to the floor on his front legs, he smashed into me and sent me flying toward the front of the room. Fighting for balance, my tail whirled as I sailed through the air. Managing to right myself, I landed on my paws and simultaneously crouched to face the tawny wolf.

My upper lip pulled back as I growled and circled around him. He did the same. We moved around like mirror images of each other.

Heel, you filthy creature, his voice echoed inside my head.

No! You heel. I owe you no allegiance.

I had no idea where that had come from, but it was true enough. He was a mean bastard who had agreed to teach me for his own selfish gains. He didn't want me here, didn't care one bit about me. His only goal was to repay Damien Ward's favor, so he could get the mage off his back.

Eric swatted in my direction, his sharp claws missing my snout by a mere inch. I jumped and swatted in return, except I didn't miss and managed to cut a gash on the side of his face. He snarled, eyes flashing with anger. He flexed his legs ready to jump.

Heel, I commanded, putting all the will I possessed behind the word.

Eric didn't jump and instead continued circling around me, looking for an angle of attack. We circled each other for a long time, issuing alternating commands to heel and stay back.

After what felt like forever, he shook his head and blinked, taking a few steps backward. Without warning, his body rippled, shifting back into its human form, his clothes settling into place as his magical shifting ring did its work.

Seeing him shift from his beautiful wolf form to a human dressed in a set of baggy sweats put a damper on my anger and brought me back into the moment. I blinked at my surroundings, realizing that I didn't want to kill Eric Cross. Not really. He was a bastard, but he was also my teacher, and I was going to need him for a few more days.

Eric leaned casually against the wall. "Lesson over," he said.

Huh?

"Don't be so dense, Sunder. I just showed you how you can use your alpha abilities to avoid a fight. You're welcome."

CHAPTER 7

Three breakfast burritos later, I arrived at the office with Rosalina. I was still staying in her place since I hadn't had a chance to move all my stuff to my condo. But, today after work, the plan was to pack it all up in the Camaro to begin settling in tonight.

I was excited, and it seemed to be the only thing able to put a smile on my face. The thought of anything else triggered my anger, including my next task, which seemed to be hanging over my head like a sharp guillotine.

Off with her head. That was what Aaron Blackridge would say when he found out his mate was dying due to rhabo. He would be here at 10 AM to talk, and I was dreading it. I was about to walk into my office when Rosalina made a face.

"Uh-oh," she said from the chair at her desk. She was looking through the window at something outside. I followed her gaze.

Jake was headed this way from across the street.

A smile stretched my lips as I geared up for the big reveal. "Watch this."

Rosalina jumped to her feet, looking scared. "Watch what? What do you mean?"

"I didn't put on Damien's poop perfume this morning."

"Oh, shit!"

The door chimed as Jake walked in. He was in shirtsleeves, jeans, boots, and a leather bracelet I'd never seen on him before. Immediately, his silver eyes opened wide, and his nose twitched, scenting the air. He turned his attention to Rosalina, nostrils flaring. When he realized the smell wasn't coming from her, his attention slowly switched to me.

My smile grew and also the feeling of satisfaction at seeing him so confused.

But his puzzlement quickly morphed into anger, and he marched in my direction like an angry bull ready to bump me into next week. At the sight of his rage, a sudden jolt of fear plunged down my spine, and I took a step back, for a second regretting my decision to reveal myself this way. He grabbed me by the shoulders, squeezing hard.

"Who did you sleep with?!" he demanded.

Huh? That threw me for a loop. Not what I was expecting. He thought my new wolfish scent came from someone I'd slept with? That was actually a thing? Suddenly, I was thinking back to all the times I'd seen him since he'd returned and realized that every single time he'd smelled of himself—just pine and rain. My heart did a little jig.

"Um, I think I hear a latte calling my name from across the street." Rosalina squeezed around the desk and quickly vacated the office, leaving me alone with a very upset werewolf.

"Answer me?!" he said, a note of desperation in his voice.

"Get your hands off me, *Jakie*." The nickname that Allison had called him seemed to piss him off even more. His mouth twisted in a sneer.

I tried to get free from his grip, but he wouldn't let me go. Instead, he pushed me against the wall and bore down on me, his face sharpening to wild angles, pupils enlarging, fangs glinting in his mouth.

"I owe you no explanation," I spat, my anger swelling to match his.

He shook his head, breathing hard, some internal battle raging inside him as if he wanted to stop his crazy behavior but couldn't. His wild side seemed to win, and he growled another command.

"Tell me, so I can kill him."

"I can sleep with whomever I want. I could even get engaged, and it would be none of your business, you two-faced bastard." I pushed against his hard chest, but moving a building would've been easier.

"*I* haven't slept with anybody else." His voice trembled with ill-contained fury. "Not since the last time I was with you."

The revelation washed over me like a bucket of cold water, leaving me with my jaw hanging open. Jake stepped away from me and raked his clawed fingers into his hair. He looked at a loss for a moment, then regret entered his gaze, probably wishing that, in his anger, he hadn't just dropped this bomb.

Seeing his vulnerability, my eyes opened to the truth. He couldn't control himself any more than I could. This dumb attraction was mutual, all the way to the inability to find any real connection with anyone else. He was as doomed to this love as I was. My satisfaction in causing him pain turned to dust, and I decided to match him bomb for bomb.

"I haven't slept with anybody else either," I said, my voice gentle.

"Don't lie." The anger returned to his silver eyes, causing his pupils to grow huge. "I can smell it on you."

"It's not what you think," I said. "Not at all."

Slowly, I lifted a hand. It shook as I held it in front of him. I willed my claws to unsheath. My fingertips itched and felt tight, but they didn't come.

Jake watched me with disgust as if I'd been tainted somehow.

"Dammit, Red! Just let me show him."

The anger did the trick, and claws sprang from my fingertips, along with soft, brown fur. At the sight of it, Jake staggered backward, his face a mask of pure shock.

"What… what…" But he couldn't find the words. He just stared at my clawed fingers as if they belonged to some horrific creature.

I jerked my hand away and hid it behind my back, feeling self-conscious and embarrassed. An absurd thought entered my mind. Did he not like his own kind? Had he only liked me because I *wasn't* a werewolf? This possibility had never occurred to me. My heart squeezed painfully as his rejection hit me like a punch to the face.

"What happened to you? What kind of curse is that?"

Curse? *Witchlights*, he thought someone had cursed me!

Well, there was only one way to relieve him of his messed up, thick-headed deduction.

Screw it, Red. I don't even like this outfit.

My wolf shuddered with pleasure, and without waiting for even a second, she took control and reveled in disclosing herself. My dress ripped down my back and fell away with the rest of my clothes. Tatters of fabric fluttered to the floor.

When the shift was done an instant later, I shook my head and inhaled Jake's scent as if for the first time. It slithered into me like a delicious poison, seeping slowly into my veins and traveling to every corner of my untamed body. I shuddered with pleasure, finding such delirious comfort in him.

I was made for him, and he was made for me. There was no denying it.

"Toni," his deep voice caused a chill to run from the top of my spine to the tip of my tail.

I lowered my head in assent.

"How… how is this possible?" Tears wavered in his eyes, something I had never seen.

I whimpered and took a step closer. He became unhinged and collapsed to his knees in front of me. His eyes held mine, looking deep into my soul. I had felt touched by him so many times, but this was completely different. It was like the inevitability of gravity, the friction of tectonic plates, the meeting of two planets that had been scheduled for collision for millions of years.

I leaned my head forward, and he slowly rested his forehead on mine. The tears that had pooled in his eyes fell, splattering silently onto his angular cheekbones.

There were no words to be said. All we could do was steep in the knowledge of each other, and the truth of what we were. And for the first time, we understood that what we felt for each other couldn't be stopped, no matter how hard we tried.

Our love hadn't been an accident. It was meant to be.

CHAPTER 8

Jake was still speechless, and all he seemed able to do was play with his leather bracelet. It was brown, about an inch thick, with a metal motif in the shape of an arrow. It reminded me of the new tattoo he'd gotten around his left biceps, an arrow that wrapped around his arm's circumference. It was nice.

I had explained everything, leaving no detail out. Almost. I still had to tell him that I was an alpha, but I was afraid about what that could mean, and not for the first time, I wished I understood more about his world, wished that I would have grown up knowing all the little nuances that came with being a werewolf.

We were in my office, Jake sitting across from me. I had fetched a pair of sweats and a T-shirt from the loft, not the best office look, but I was my own boss, so screw it.

He rubbed his forehead, looking overwhelmed.

A nervous flutter started building in my stomach. "Say something, Jake."

"I don't know what to say."

"There's only one thing I really want to know, so maybe you

can answer this… does this change anything for us?"

His grave expression didn't budge as he peered up to meet my gaze. I felt my heart squeeze painfully because what I perceived in his features didn't give me any hope.

"Who is your father, Toni?" he asked.

Huh? I did a double-take. This was what he chose to talk about?

"What does that matter?" I asked, my irrational anger making my voice quiver.

"Just tell me who he is."

I set my jaw and refused to answer for a few beats. At last, I said, "I don't know."

One of Jake's eyes twitched. "How can you not know? Your mother didn't tell you?"

"No, she didn't volunteer the information, and I didn't care to find out."

"You didn't care to find out?!" He sounded appalled.

"I was too busy mourning for my dad. You knew him, Jake, and you saw how close we were, how much I loved him. I don't want any other father but him."

"You have to find out who sired you." His statement rang with finality as if no other alternative existed—especially the one I preferred.

"Why is it so important? Why did you ask that instead of answering my question?"

Jake stood and walked to the door. I thought he would leave, but he stopped at the threshold and looked out into the lobby. "I want to know if he belongs to one of the local packs."

I thought for a moment, then understood his angle. "You're worried he's a member of an enemy pack, is that it?"

He turned to face me. "Yes. But… I don't guess it matters either way."

"Because…"

"Because this…" He paused. "This doesn't change anything."

I stood up abruptly, making my chair roll back and crash against the wall. "How can you say that? You feel it as well as I do. We're meant for each other, Jake. You can't marry that insipid woman."

"I can't break the pact."

"Pact? What pact?"

"My grandfather and Craig Blackridge have agreed for our packs to join. My grandfather stepped down as alpha in favor of Blackridge, with the condition that once I marry Allison I will become pack leader. It strengthens our position against Ulfen Erickson's and Travis Hillworth's packs."

The Blackridges, Knights, Ericksons, and Hillworths were the four biggest packs in St. Louis and had been for generations.

"We've reached a consensus through," Jake hesitated, "through an unbreakable pact. I can't back down."

"An *unbreakable* pact?"

He nodded. "Magic was involved."

"There has to be a way out. Tell them you changed your mind."

"It doesn't work that way, Toni. If any party breaks the pact, it would be a death sentence."

"What?! That's stupid. Who would agree to something like that?"

"It's the way packs do things."

"How could you?"

"Toni," he turned and walked in my direction, raising a hand as if to touch me.

I pointed at him with a shaky finger. "Stay away from me. Don't come any closer. I don't need your pity."

He shook his head and opened his mouth to argue.

"Don't deny it. I see it in your face. You feel sorry for me because I still don't matter."

"That's not true."

I laughed with scorn. "Isn't it, though? Tell me this, would it have made a difference if you'd known before your stupid pact?"

He hesitated for a moment too long.

"I guess I'm *that* irrelevant."

"You're not irrelevant, Toni," he said emphatically. "I love you."

"And what difference does that make in your screwed-up world?"

He had no answer for that. He was caught up in something much bigger than what he felt for me. The knowledge hurt me deeply.

That vindictive streak that caused me to leave my wolf scent exposed this morning came back with a vengeance. A cold, calculating smile stretched my lips.

"Do you know what's the cherry on top? The thing that will erase any doubt from your mind about whether or not we can be together?"

He frowned, a flash of fear clouding his expression for a moment.

"I'm not just any werewolf, Jake. I'm an alpha."

He scanned me through narrowed eyes. I held steady through his scrutiny, then with a careless push I forced my thoughts into his mind.

I guess I wasn't made for you after all.

My anger thrilled through us like a living thing. Jake's face crumpled, revealing the pain he felt at the discovery. Just moments ago, the world had seemed perfect, made for us to conquer together, and now, so quickly, I'd learned that fate was playing a game with me, and I was the freaking ball everyone loved to hit out of the park.

"It does seem that way," he said, slowly retreating out of the office. "I wish things were different. I came to apologize for not telling you about the engagement. It happened quickly and I didn't have a chance. I didn't want you to find out the way you did. I wanted to tell you myself." He chuckled sadly and gestured toward his office. "Perhaps, I should move out, after all. It's not wise for me to have my office so close to yours. Maybe, you would like to expand, knock down a few walls and take over the place. I'm nearly done with all the repairs."

"Get out of here, Jake. There's no room for such niceties between us."

He hung his head, sadness weighing him down. "If you ever need me…"

I was about to tell him to go to hell, when the front door chimed open and steps rushed in. Jake glanced over, his expression turning to worry.

"What's the matter?" he asked as he moved out of the way and Rosalina rushed into my office.

My heart started pounding at the sight of her panicked expression. She held her cell phone and stared at it for a moment before she managed to say a word.

"Dani just called. She couldn't reach you."

I looked at my phone, which lay face down on the desk. I had turned it off so I could explain everything to Jake without interruption. My legs turned rubbery. For my oldest sister to have called Rosalina something really bad must've happened.

"Is she all right?"

Rosalina nodded. "Dani is fine. It's your mother. She's been attacked."

CHAPTER 9

The Camaro's tires screeched as I turned into an open parking spot in front of St. Mary's Hospital. I jumped out of the car and headed toward the front door at full pelt. I ignored Jake as he parked his motorcycle next to my car. He'd wanted to ride with me, but I pushed him away as soon as Rosalina told me where to find my mother. I didn't want him here, but he seemed bent on inserting himself into the situation regardless of my wishes. He was a thorn —no a stake—in my side, and I was a masochist.

I followed the signs toward the emergency room, dodging people as I ran down the brightly lit corridor. In the waiting area, my eyes immediately homed in on my sisters. Dani and Lucia were sitting next to each other, staring at the floor, their faces etched with concern.

Lucia sensed me first and glanced up. I ran toward her, and she jumped to her feet and wrapped me in a tight hug. Tears flowed freely down my cheeks. The last time I'd seen my mother I'd been so mean to her, so inflexible and unforgiving, and now…

God, please let her be all right.

I pushed my baby sister to arm's length. "How is she?"

Lucia was unable to answer and glanced at Dani, who seemed in better control of her emotions.

"She'll be fine," Dani said, her tone reassuring, professional, as if she were speaking about one of her own patients.

"Are you sure?"

"Yes, I know one of the doctors, and I talked to her before they took Mom to the operating room. She said Mom will be okay."

The big pressure that had built and built in my chest on my way here released a little, and suddenly I could breathe much more easily.

Dani's and Lucia's gazes drifted over my shoulder, and without glancing back, I knew Jake was there. His scent and presence felt like a north to my adrift life. I resisted the urge to whirl around and tell him to leave. I needed to sever our bond once and for all, but how?

Doing my best to ignore him, I took a deep breath and asked my next question. "What happened?"

This time it was Dani's turn to defer to Lucia.

"I was late for school," my little sister said, "and Mom was going to drive me there. We were leaving the house when this huge black wolf came out of nowhere."

My heart stopped as she spoke and related everything that had happened. Jake moved closer and stood next to me, his full attention on my sister.

"I saw the wolf in time," Lucia continued, "and told Mom to run. I hurled my backpack at it and turned tail after Mom. It all happened so fast. She was slow, and the wolf was coming. I used my powers to hurl a couple of Mom's potted plants backwards. You know the ones she keeps on the porch, but I did it without looking back. I was just so panicked, I didn't know what I was doing."

"It's okay, Luce." Dani rubbed our little sister's back. "It's okay. You did good."

Lucia had strong telekinetic abilities. She had once made a tornado of toys in her room when she got mad at me for drawing a poop emoji on her coloring book. She could be scary.

She shook her head, tears pooling in her eyes. "No, I didn't. She could have died because I wasn't brave enough. I should have turned around and faced that bastard. But Mom tripped on the porch steps and fell, and he jumped on her and bit her."

She wrapped her arms protectively around her stomach, horror rippling from her like a wave, hitting me with its powerful quality and making me feel as if I'd been there.

"Who was it? Do you know him?" Jake asked, his voice like the calm before the storm.

"No, but," her tone turned bitter and angry, "I hope werewolves can't grow back their eyeballs."

My eyebrows went up. What had Lucia managed to do?

"She used her skill and sent a garden weeder straight into the wolf's eye," Dani said. "It gave her enough time to pull Mom into the house and shut the door. The protective spells kept the beast from coming in."

Lucia was crying, big fat tears sliding down her cheeks.

"Luce," I said, squeezing her hand. "Dani's right, you did great. You saved Mom."

But she pulled her hand from mine, unwilling to believe she'd done enough to help her. She sat back down and crossed her arms, closing herself off.

"It doesn't make any sense," Dani said. "Who could have attacked her?" She searched my face, and I noticed a hint of accusation in her eyes—not that I could blame her. We'd just discovered I was a werewolf, and the next thing we knew, one was trying to kill our mother.

Worst of all… she was right. This was my fault.

I turned to Jake. "It was Blake."

He nodded, fully in agreement.

"Who?" Dani asked.

"It's a long story," I said.

"I have time."

"I'll tell you everything, but I should call Tom. He needs to know, and he may be able to provide some protection for you and Mom."

"What's going on, Toni? Are you in some kind of trouble?"

That was when I realized that, without thinking things through, I had dug myself deeper into this mess than I'd imagined. Up to now, I'd believed myself to be on the fringes of this clusterfuck, but in truth, I was in the thick of it. I'd messed with the wrong werewolf. Blake was savage and vindictive, and he had it in for me.

ꕥ

Five hours later, they had moved Mom from the recovery area to a regular room. Dani and Lucia led the way in as they allowed us to see her for the first time.

I hung back by the door while they walked ahead of me.

"Mom!" Lucia exclaimed and hugged her awkwardly, making sure not to hurt her.

"Oh, sweetheart, I was so worried about you," Mom said, smoothing her younger daughter's hair.

Dani laughed. "Leave it to you to be worried about us while you're the one in the hospital." She kissed Mom on the forehead.

"I'm so glad you're all right."

"The doctor said I'll be right as rain in a couple of days. She said there won't even be a scar. I'll still be able to wear my bikini."

Dani laughed.

And Lucia made a face. "Ew, now I won't be able to get that image out of my head."

Mom looked sallow and exhausted, her eyelids drooping heavily as if she were on the verge of falling asleep. Her hair lay limp against her head. She looked nothing like the polished lady who didn't go anywhere without makeup and a nice hair-do.

I took a step forward, and Mom finally noticed me.

She pressed a hand to her mouth, her eyes immediately filling with tears. "You're here," she sobbed.

I took a few tentative steps toward her, then rushed into her arms, pressing my face to hers, letting the relief wash over me and pushing away all the anger I'd harbored in my heart since the day I found out she'd lied to me.

"Oh, honey, I have missed you so much," she said.

I spoke through the lump in my throat. "If something had happened to you—"

"*Shh*, I'm all right. I'm right here."

"I'm sorry I've been so angry at you."

"I deserved it. I should have never lied to you."

We cried in each other's arms, both relieved in our own way. When I finally pulled away, I was ready to tell her and my sisters everything. They needed to know what they were up against, so they could keep their eyes open.

"It's all my fault," I said.

Mom frowned, confused.

"It wasn't some random attack, Mom. That wolf that came after you, I know him. His name is Blake Foster."

"Wait," Dani said, "isn't that the same guy they killed a few weeks ago, the one hanging from his neck at one of Ulfen Erickson's charity functions."

I nodded. "He isn't dead, and now, he has a vendetta against me."

"Nice," Lucia said, her voice dripping with sarcasm.

"But we'll take care of him," Jake said, appearing behind me, carrying a cardboard holder with three coffees.

"Oh, my savior!" Lucia snatched a coffee, unbalancing the holder.

Jake's quick reflexes kicked in, and he managed to gracefully offer Dani the next cup. When he turned to me, I took it begrudgingly.

"Mrs. Sunder," Jake inclined his head, "I'm pleased to see you're all right. I didn't get you a coffee because I figured you wouldn't be allowed to drink it."

"Jacob Knight." Mom raised her eyebrows and regarded him appreciatively. "I'd heard you were back in town. Though, if I hadn't, maybe the unexpected wolf attack would have clued me in."

Jake winced but said nothing.

"Mom, this is not his fault," I said.

"Isn't it though?" I got the feeling she wanted to say more, but given that we'd just reconciled and she didn't know where Jake and I stood, she refrained.

Dani, as always, became the voice of reason. "I don't think this is anyone else's fault but Blake Foster's."

No one could argue with that. He didn't have to be such a psycho killer. Next time I saw him, *I* was going to kill *him*.

Lucia sipped her coffee, smacked her lips, then asked, "And how do you plan to take care of that *effing* bastard, *Mr. Knight*?"

"Language, Lucia." Mom scowled.

My little sister rolled her eyes. "I said *effing*, Mom."

"You did. And also used the 'b' word."

"Whatever."

"Just wait 'till I'm out of this bed, young lady."

Lucia ignored the threat and gave Jake a pointed glare.

"I have already been looking into his whereabouts, and I have a few leads," Jake said.

I paused with my cup halfway to my lips. "You do?"

Jake's eyes locked with mine. "You don't worry about it. Take care of your Mom, and I'll take care of Blake." He bowed respectfully. "Ladies, I'm glad you're all safe. Good day."

I wanted to follow after him and demand that he keep me in the loop, but since I didn't want my family to worry, I did the next best thing.

You tell me if you find him, I spoke in his mind using my alpha skills.

I sensed a grunt from him and nothing else. As I shook my head with irritation, I noticed Lucia leaning forward to check out his ass. I slapped her shoulder, heat climbing up my neck at her audacity.

She rolled her eyes, her favorite pastime. "You're all such prudes."

Moments later, two policemen appeared at the door with instructions from Detective Freeman to guard the patient and make sure she got home safely. It gave me some peace of mind, but I wouldn't feel completely at ease until Blake was behind bars.

Or better yet, dead.

CHAPTER 10

"Thank the witchlights your mom is okay," Rosalina said when I got to the agency an hour later. I had gone to her condo to change from my sweats into a pair of black slacks with a matching jacket and blouse.

She was also wearing a different outfit, which was strange. "Did you change?" I asked.

"Um, yeah." She glanced at her teal dress. "I spilled coffee on the other one and ran home real quick to put this on."

Odd. She was a pro at getting out stains with some handy wipes she kept in her desk. It must have been the mother of all stains.

Rosalina had rescheduled our appointment with Aaron Blackridge and had held down the fort while I was gone, yet again. I smiled gratefully at her, wondering if her patience would run out soon. My life had gotten too complicated, and things were nothing like they had been when we got started. I had to get my act together. This wasn't fair to her. Not at all.

She handed me a manila folder with Aaron's name stamped on it, her fingers letting go of it a bit reluctantly.

"I'm sorry," I said. "This is all my fault."

"We have other customers lined up. It'll be all right," she said, sounding more chipper than she looked.

The door chimed and Aaron walked in. He wore a black T-shirt with a splash of color and musical notes scattered around. His skinny jeans were stuffed into shoes that looked like something I could wear in space. They were bright blue and really cool.

He greeted us with a smile, which quickly disappeared. "What's this about? You got me a bit worried since you said it was important."

"It is." I extended a hand toward our small sitting area. He sat, and we took our positions across from him, the coffee table between us. "How is Josh?"

"He's great. We've been getting to know each other, and all I can say is that… he's perfect." He beamed, his gaze sparkling with happiness.

I tried to smile, but instead, I felt like crying.

Aaron was perceptive enough and noticed my distress. "What's wrong?"

"I'm afraid I have some bad news to give you."

He straightened, his jaw setting, the friendliness in his expression disappearing.

"After we introduced you to Josh, we found out that… he's not well."

His eyes danced around, betraying his confusion. He sputtered a laugh. "Not well? He's a vampire. Vampires are always well." Then he gasped, his eyes widening, as he seemed to realize something. "He's… he's taking rhabo."

Rosalina pressed a hand to her chest as we exchanged a glance. I was surprised he'd figured it out so quickly.

"You know about rhabo then," I said. "I just recently learned about it. If I had known that Josh's health was compromised, I would have never…" I let the words hang and set the manila folder on the coffee table. "This is a full refund for our services. There is no apology we can offer to make this better. Please know that we don't give this back as any sort of reparation—we know there is nothing that can undo the pain this will cause—but it does not feel right to take it."

Aaron stared at the folder, tears pooling in his dark eyes. "It can't be. He looks fine. He's happy. We're happy. You must be wrong." He glanced up, a hint of hope etching his features.

"I don't believe I am," I said. "But he's the only one who can let you know for sure."

He swatted a tear from his face and swallowed audibly. "If he's sick, I'll move heaven and earth to make him better. He'll be all right."

I wanted to tell him that I would do the same—move heaven and earth *and* entire realms if necessary—to help undo the pain I'd caused, that I was already trying to convince a powerful mage to give me some of the healing elixir he planned to create. But I didn't have anything concrete, so why give him false hopes?

"We are very sorry, Mr. Blackridge," Rosalina said, her tone sincere and repentant.

Aaron shook his head. "I would never blame you." His voice trembled a little as he spoke. "I want you to know that. I appreciate you letting me know. You could have ignored this, turned a blind eye, but I see you have ethics." He stood. "I'll go now. I need to talk to Josh." He started walking away without taking the folder, which contained his uncashed check for the second part of his payment, as well as a check from us, returning his deposit.

I picked it up and offered it to him. "Please, take this."

He shook his head. "You did your job. I have no complaints."

"I insist."

He took it reluctantly. "I understand. Thank you."

After he left, Rosalina and I slumped in our chairs.

"I think this is the hardest thing we've ever had to do since we opened the agency," she said.

"Damn right it is."

I didn't want to have to do anything like that ever again.

CHAPTER 11

The next day was just as long and tiring as the previous. It started with training with Eric, my second to last session. We ran in the woods where he taught me to follow a trail using my sharp nose and keen eyes. He also spent some time teaching me a few tricks to use during fights, things like how to never expose my tender belly, how to use my tail for balance and feigning, and how to push and slice an opponent with my back legs if I fell.

At the office, we had a long day, contacting prospective customers, and doing a talk at a singles group explaining the benefits of a true mate versus an accidental one. We left our brochures behind, hoping that some of them might take the plunge and hire us.

Celina Morelli and Aaron Blackridge had been our only high profile customers so far. We were hoping for some more word-of-mouth business coming from them, but it wasn't happening as fast as we would've liked, and in truth, we didn't think Aaron would comfortably recommend us to anyone—no matter what he thought about our ethics. We had screwed up his life. Royally. And even if he didn't think so, his friends probably would.

Being a glutton for punishment, I went to kick-boxing class and got my ass thoroughly exhausted. So at the end of the day, feeling as achy as if I'd been mugged and beaten, I keyed the lock to my condo and walked in. Rosalina had wanted me to go home with her since I still hadn't moved any of my stuff over, but I was looking forward to a quiet night without expectations of any kind.

I walked into my bedroom and dropped my duffel bag on the floor. The mattress was still bare, but I had brought new sheets and a few other necessities for my first night at home.

After ordering some take-out, I made the bed and quickly realized I'd forgotten to bring a pillow. But I was so exhausted, I doubted I would even notice once I laid my head down. After that, I hung a shower curtain in the bathroom. Its vinyl smell impregnated the place, making my nose wrinkle.

That's what you get for buying the cheapest liner available.

I put my one towel on the shelf, unwrapped a bar of soap, and set my toothbrush and toothpaste on the counter. It was all simple and basic, but I felt empowered all the same. Everything in the condo was mine, bought with my own money.

When the bell rang, I answered the door without looking. My stomach was growling at the thought of my juicy burger, but when I opened the door something much taller than the triple-decker I'd ordered was waiting for me.

"Jake," I blinked in surprise, "what are you doing here? How did you know where to find me?"

"Rosalina told me."

I'm going to kill her, I thought.

Don't do that, Jake thought back.

Damn, I hadn't meant to think that so loudly.

Jake shrugged. "Rosalina only told me because I twisted her arm."

"You'd better not have laid a finger on her."

"I meant that in the figurative sense, of course. May I come in?"

I put a hand on my hip. "Nope. You're not welcome here."

He opened his mouth to say something when steps sounded behind him. He abruptly turned, crouching low, ready to attack.

I rolled my eyes. "Don't be stupid. It's just my dinner."

A pimply guy carrying a large paper bag stopped on a dime, staring wide-eyed at the threatening man standing in the way of his delivery.

I sighed in frustration. "Get in, Jake."

He crossed the threshold but kept an eye on the guy, who stayed as far away as possible as he handed over the bag. I took it, and he whirled and left in a hurry. I closed the door and stared up at Jake. Tall and imposing, he stood in the little foyer.

So much for my quiet evening.

I took my dinner to the living room, set it up on the coffee table, and sat cross legged on the floor.

Jake glanced around. "I like the new place."

I made a sound in the back of my throat as I took my first bite and pretty much ignored him. He walked around the armchair across from me and sat, watching me closely. He gave my burger and onion rings a hungry look. His stomach growled, and he licked his lips.

Picking up one of the crunchy rings, I took a bite, rolling my eyes into the back of my head and making a moan of pleasure. I followed that with a big slurp of my strawberry shake.

"Mm, that hits the spot," I practically moaned, sounding like I'd just had an orgasm.

He pursed his lips and rubbed his chin, judging me hard. "I

guess I should've grabbed dinner before I headed here. Didn't think you'd be so inhospitable."

"I'm not running a restaurant or a soup kitchen here. Hell, I don't even have anything in my fridge, so if you're hungry, make this quick and hit the road."

"Maybe I made a mistake coming here." He stood and started walking toward the door. "I just thought you might want to know that I found Blake."

"Wait, what?!" I jumped to my feet, my dinner forgotten. "Where is he?"

He glanced over his shoulder and gave me a crooked smile. "I'll tell you… if you share your burger. I haven't eaten all day. Been busy, tracking the bastard and storing him in a safe place."

"Storing him?"

"Yeah, he's waiting for us." As he said this, his voice rang with malice, making me wonder what he had in mind.

I gestured toward my burger. "You can have it all. The rings and shake will hold me."

Jake swaggered back toward the armchair and sat. Smiling as if he'd gotten away with murder, he slid the burger his way and began eating. He devoured the whole thing in a few bites.

I watched him closely, wondering if this was a good time to tell him about Stephen. He needed to know that the man he called his friend might be the son of a bitch behind the impending war between vampires and werewolves. But would he believe me? Maybe it would be better if I got the truth out of Blake instead.

Jake patted his stomach. "That was better than the pizza I had earlier."

I stopped mid-chew. "I thought you said you hadn't eaten anything all day."

"I lied. You were enjoying that far too much. I couldn't allow that."

"You're a bastard."

"I've been called that more than once." He dropped his satisfied smile and grew serious. "I came because I got a sense that you wanted to settle the score with Blake, but you don't have to come with me. I can take care of it."

"Oh, I'm coming with you." My voice was a chilling whisper that made Jake peer at me closely. He looked surprised and worried when he noticed my expression.

My seething anger had worked itself to a boil at the thought of taking revenge on Blake for what he'd done to my mother. The bastard would pay.

It seemed I finally had a good use for my rage.

CHAPTER 12

Crickets chirped loudly, and a waning crescent moon hung high in the sky. Jake walked in front of me, his boots crunching leaves and branches without care. Tall trees loomed above us, some of their branches almost bare as leaves were only beginning to sprout. It was a cool fifty-eight degrees, nice for a walk in the woods.

I glanced around, feeling a dreadful sense of déjà vu.

"Wait," I said, "I know this place. This is where we found Emily Garner, isn't it?"

"It is."

The perverted vampire who had kidnapped the little girl had brought her here and left her tied up in a cave, hoping to eat her for dessert after a night of hunting in the city. Except, I had tracked her just in time, and Jake and I rushed here to save her.

I shivered at the memory. We had almost been too late, and only Jake's werewolf speed had stopped the vamp from harming her. The monster had been poised to drain her dry when we entered the cave. Jake leaped on him, clamped his jaws around his neck, and hurled him against the cave's rock wall. The vamp had been no match for Jake, though the blood leech rose from the ground to attack me and raked his claws across my stomach before Jake did him in for good.

Up ahead, the outline of a craggy hill appeared. My body began tingling with anticipation, and my wolf stirred restlessly under my skin, ready to burst out into the open.

The cave's mouth was pitch dark. An edge of fear sliced through me, and I went for my cell phone, thinking of turning on the flashlight. The cave was shallow, and dim moonlight seeped into it, enough for my werewolf eyes to see by. I let the phone be.

Jake walked ahead of me, holding up an arm to pause me long enough to look into the cave and make sure it was safe to go in. After a quick check, he put his arm down and I followed.

Blake was kneeling on the rocky ground, straining against two thick chains anchored to the wall. His right eye was swollen shut, making me wonder if my little sister had truly succeeded in putting it out for good. Black veins stretched across his chest, a sign that he had wolfsbane in his system, the poison Jake had used to subdue him and get him here. Sweat dripped down his forehead and bare chest. Clearly, he'd been fighting to get free.

"I told you not to waste your time trying to escape. Those chains are special," Jake sneered.

"You fucking bastard. You will pay for this."

"I think you got this all wrong. You're the one building up debt, attacking helpless women when your beef is with us."

Blake spat on the ground. "She tasted like shit."

That rage that was becoming so familiar flared up inside my gut. I stepped forward and slapped him across the face, leaving behind four deep scratch marks. My claws had unsheathed of their own accord, and I'd carved him up like a turkey. He hissed in pain.

"You don't mess with my family." I grabbed his face in my hand and squeezed hard. "Maybe I'll finish what my sister started." I pressed the tip of a long sharp claw to the corner of his eye.

Blake tried to pull away, but I held him steady, slowly increasing the pressure against his lower eyelid. His chest started pumping as his breathing became agitated.

I felt his fear like a puddle of urine spreading underfoot. My nose twitched recognizing its acrid smell for what it was. Like when he'd thought he was dying from that poisoned bullet, Blake's cowardice poured out of him like sickening pus from a wound.

"You're pathetic," I said, as my claw pierced his skin and a bead of blood welled up beneath his eye.

"Don't do it," he begged. "I'll be blind."

So Lucia *had* succeeded in removing his other eyeball, and there was nothing under that swollen mess. Good.

"It would be no less than you deserve." I increased the pressure, the scent of his blood piercing my nostrils as a small streak slid down his cheek.

Jake took a step closer, moving into my field of vision. I cut a glance in his direction and sensed his disapproval. The note of surprise in his eyes gave me pause. Taken aback, I released Blake and pulled away. Suddenly feeling dirty, I wiped my hands off on my jeans, getting rid of Blake's foul stench.

Blake slumped forward, sinking to his knees with relief. Jake nodded, also looking relieved. I pressed my fist to my mouth, my heart pounding in my chest, the scent of blood stirring my anger. Images of Blake's mutilated face flashed before my eyes as I imagined what I could do to him.

No! That's not me.

I wasn't the kind of person that plucked people's eyeballs out. What was happening to me?

I thought it must be Red, but I had started to feel so intertwined with my wolf that it was getting difficult to tell where one began and the other one ended.

"She's pissed at you, and it's her right to be," Jake said. "I don't want her to get her hands dirty with the likes of you, but I don't have any qualms about my own hands touching filth. So how about you start talking and tell us who saved you at the warehouse?"

Blake's lone eye swiveled to contemptuously peer up at Jake. He pressed his mouth into a thin line and said nothing.

"That's big posturing for a big coward like you." Jake cracked his knuckles, then, without warning, delivered a right hook to Blake's jaw.

His head snapped to one side, the crack of bone against bone resonating in the cave, sending images of the man I'd seen Blake kill in the warehouse flickering before my eyes. The horror of what I'd witnessed washed over me all over again. Without thinking, I laid a hand on Jake's shoulder as he prepared to deliver another punch.

"Stop," I said.

"Maybe you should wait outside." He nodded towards the cave's entrance.

"I don't want you getting your hands dirty either."

Jake opened his mouth to argue, but I pulled him by the arm and dragged him outside, well out of Blake's earshot. The thought of making Blake pay hadn't seemed so unpalatable until his stink had transferred to us. If we killed him, we would become just like him. Nothing could be worse.

"We should turn him in," I said.

The wind blew, rustling the leaves above us. A shiver ran up my spine, reminding me of Jake's warm embrace, making me crave for it.

"This is our chance to find out who else is behind all of this," he argued. "If we turn him in to the police, they'll probably let him go, just like they let Jenson Boyle go."

He wasn't wrong about that, but it had just occurred to me that maybe pretending *not* to know gave us an advantage. "I think I already know who Blake works for."

Jake frowned. "How?"

"While he was twisting in pain at the warehouse after I shot him with the wolfsbane, he called out for help, not knowing that I could hear him."

"Shit! You've known all along, and you didn't tell me? Why?"

"Let me ask you something," I said, avoiding his question, wanting to get a last bit of information to give me the assurance I'd been lacking. "Had you seen Stephen's wolf before that day Jenson attacked us at the restaurant?"

"Why would you ask me that?"

"Well, had you?"

"No. there was never an occasion for it." He paused and considered for a moment. "You're not trying to tell me that…"

"Blake called out for Stephen's help."

"No." He shook his head. "It can't be."

"I think he was there, Jake. He was the second wolf that attacked you. He wiped out the security footage and helped Blake escape."

His eyes darted over the underbrush. "That wolf was russet-colored, not brown like Stephen was in the restaurant."

"His coloring wouldn't be something hard to disguise with magic."

"But that would mean that… he kidnapped himself and put his own father in jail. He wouldn't…" He trailed off, his clear eyes wandering about some more as he thought about this new information.

"I don't want to believe it either," I said, "but I know what I heard."

"I'm sorry, but I need more proof than that. Stephen is my friend."

"I've told Freeman about it. He says there are things about Stephen's kidnapping that don't add up. He's looking into it, and I'm sure he'll find something. Maybe that'll be proof enough for you."

"If this is true…" His upper lip twitched, then he shook his head. "I'll look into it."

I nodded, glad that he was willing to consider the possibility. "I'll call Tom and tell him we got Blake. In case Stephen is really behind all of this, I think it's best if he doesn't know we suspect him."

"Okay," Jake agreed, though not without reluctance.

I turned and started moving away from Jake. He walked behind me. The terrain was rocky and uneven. For balance, I put my hands out, and he came up behind me and placed a hand on my waist, offering me extra support. His touch was electrifying as always. I stopped abruptly. He stopped too, the length of his torso pressed against my back. I didn't move for a few beats, and simply enjoyed his warmth, his strong presence.

He leaned closer and inhaled. My eyelids fluttered.

Mine. He's mine.

The possessive feeling was stronger than ever. No one else but me had a right to his touch, his kiss, his love. It didn't matter that his grandfather had plans for him, that he had sold him to the highest bidder. Pact or no pact, his heart beat for me, and I could hear it now, speeding up to match mine.

Why should I step aside and allow anyone to take him from

me? Why should I condemn him and myself to a life of misery apart from each other? Why should I make this easy for Walter and Allison and anyone else who wanted to steal him from me?

Slowly, very slowly, I turned to face him. His hands remained on my waist even as I swiveled. He stood a mere inch from me. I placed a hand on his chest, right over his heart.

"I can hear it," I whispered, my eyes half-lidded. "Can you hear mine?"

He swallowed, his Adam's apple bobbing up and down.

I inhaled deeply. "Have I told you that my sense of smell is even better now?"

"No, you haven't."

I raised my chin and licked my lips. "You want me. I can smell your desire."

"What are you doing, Toni?"

I pressed two fingers to his mouth and let them travel gently across his lower lip. "I'm enjoying you."

My voice was deep, sensuous, charged with a confidence I'd never felt before. Jake was a master of seduction and had always taken the lead while I found myself helpless against his charms. Maybe it was my turn to repay the favor, to drive him crazy the way he'd done with me so many times.

My fingers explored his torso, enjoying the peaks and valleys, the solidity of his young strong body. On the way up, I quickly undid a couple of buttons on his shirt, then my hand climbed higher and reached the nape of his neck where his light brown hair was soft as a kitten's fur. Gently, I pulled him down, brought his lips closer to mine. He seemed to resist for an instant, but then he was helpless and complied.

"Tell me something," I said, my hot breath caressing his lips and making him shudder while my fingers undid a few more buttons without his notice. "Why should I make this easy for you? Why shouldn't I fight for you, huh?" I found the last button, made quick work of it, and his shirt fell open.

His eyes, which had been closed, sprang open, meeting mine. He was struck mute and offered no answer.

"She doesn't know you like I do, Jake." I caressed his chest, my fingers marking a gentle path down the length of his smooth, right pec. "She can't make you feel this way." I brushed my lips over his heart and trailed kisses to his collarbone, soaking in his heat, inhaling his maddening musk.

The scent of his desire engulfed me suddenly, and he captured me in his arms. One of his hands slid under my hair and pulled me closer. Our lips met in a desperate kiss. He pressed me against him, his tongue caressing mine, his teeth biting my lower lip while his other hand grabbed my ass and pressed me against him.

I raked my fingernails down his back. He hissed and pressed his mouth to my neck, nibbling, sending shudders of pleasure down my body.

My heart swelled with passion and so much more.

"I love you, Jake," I said, without thinking.

He went utterly still and pulled away, his eyes searching my face. He looked as if I'd slapped him. Turning away from me, he started buttoning his shirt.

"You can't tell me that now," he said.

I rubbed my swollen lips, aching for more of his kisses. "I love you," I repeated. "You can't pretend you didn't know that."

"I didn't. You had never said it. I thought…"

"You thought what?"

"I thought it was all physical. Desire. Then when you told me you were a werewolf, I thought I'd been right all along, that it had been no more than *cravedark*."

"What is that?"

"It happens sometimes when a male and a female instinctively know they will make strong offspring if they mate. The attraction doesn't stop until she conceives, then it's gone. But if you love me, then…"

"Then what?"

"Then I'm a dead man."

ജ്ഞ

Jake had grown dead silent, refusing to explain what he'd meant by saying he was a dead man. We stood by the side of the road. There were four police cars next to my Camaro, their lights flashing blue and red, coloring the trees and the graveled shoulder.

Three cops were pushing Blake up the embankment toward the blacktop. He fought them as if he had any chance of escaping, handcuffed and collared as he was. There was no shifting with those dampening devices on him. They possessed strong magic.

The taste of Jake's skin lingered on my lips, and for an instant, I closed my eyes and imagined my fingers sliding down his smooth chest.

Tom Freeman walked away from one of the police cars and headed in our direction. He wore a loose tie around his neck, and a long coat that flapped behind him.

"Sorry to have doubted you, kiddo. This one will rock the department, probably prompt an investigation in the coroner's office. Only God knows how they got fooled into thinking Blake was a dead man."

"Maybe he just bribed them," Jake offered.

Tom huffed. "I know the men who conducted the autopsy, and they're not the kind to take a bribe."

"My mother will press charges," I said. "Please make sure he doesn't go free like Jenson. That asshole mage has already tried to kill me again."

The detective's eyes opened wide. "You didn't mention that."

I shrugged.

"We'll get him, too," Jake said.

"About that, you can't go 'round taking the law into your own hands. It's not safe, and it's not your job, so call us instead of barging into a dangerous situation like you've been doing." He pulled out a small pad and poised a pen over it. "If you have any additional information that can help shed some light on what's going on, spill it."

"I told you everything I know," I said. "I think Stephen is behind this. I hope this time you'll believe me."

I glanced in Blake's direction, who was being stuffed into the back seat of one of the patrol cars. If Tom had believed me about Blake, maybe my mother wouldn't have been attacked. I could see by the subtle shift in the detective's expression that he got my meaning.

"Did you find anything in your case files?" I asked.

Tom shook his head. "Nothing concrete, just small loose ends that don't prove anything."

I huffed. "I'd better go, then. I have an appointment early tomorrow morning."

Jake started after me, but I turned toward him and put a hand up. "I think you'd better catch a ride with Tom. I've had enough of you for one day." I was all hot and bothered, and he didn't seem as willing as I felt. He'd turned away from me, *dammit*! I didn't need him nearby to tempt me anymore.

He looked like he was about to protest, but he only said, "Be careful."

I turned my back on him and kept walking. "Don't worry, I can take care of myself better than ever."

CHAPTER 13

"Do most werewolves marry for love?" I asked Eric almost as soon as I walked into his training room the next morning at 4 AM. It was our last training session, and I wanted all the answers.

He sighed tiredly, turned toward the mirrored wall, and straightened his pristine white T-shirt. "You've got a one track mind, Sunder. Don't tell me you're in love with Jacob Knight." He blew air through his nose as if he thought that was the most ridiculous thing in the world.

"I am," I said. "And he's in love with me."

That took the sneer right out of his face, which was saying a lot since "sneer" seemed to be his default expression.

"Did he tell you that?" he asked after a moment.

"He did."

"And did you… did you tell him how you feel about him, too?"

"Yes, and right after that, he told me he was a dead man. What did he mean? He wouldn't explain."

He considered for a moment. "You said he got engaged to

Allison Blackridge, right?"

I nodded. "Yes, and he said his grandfather made some sort of pact."

Eric considered. "Must have been a Blood Covenant then."

"A what?"

"A Blood Covenant. It's an unbreakable pact made between two or more werewolves. In this case, probably Craig Blackridge and his daughter, and Walter Knight and your Jake. Blood magic is at the heart of this type of pact, which means the participants can't back out, even if they want to. Unless they're willing to die, of course. There's usually a deadline, and if the pact isn't fulfilled in time, those who break it bite the dust."

My heart hammered as reality dawned on me.

"Commonly their death isn't pretty either," Eric added, fueling the horror that had started to fill my chest.

But if you love me, then I'm a dead man, Jake's words echoed inside my head.

"He must be planning not to go through with it," I said, thinking out loud.

"You'll have to ask *him* that."

Oh, God! What had I done? Had confessing my love for him condemned him to death?

Eric let out an aggravated breath. "Can we get on with our training?"

I shook myself, doing my best to push down the turmoil of emotions and thoughts that threatened to undo me. This was our last session. After today, Eric's agreement with Damien would be fulfilled, and Eric would be rid of me. I frowned, realizing that I would miss him.

Shit, what was wrong with me? Eric hated my guts and behaved like a complete asshat all the time. I must be a glutton for punishment.

"Sure, let's get started," I said.

Same as yesterday, we shifted, jumped out through a window, and into the forest behind his house, and began our training.

He taught me how to detect sounds and pinpoint their exact sources. Following his directions, I used my sense of hearing to find a tiny mole in its den. The scraping of claws against the deep, wet earth of its hiding place was barely audible. Yet, I was able to determine the animal's location with unerring accuracy.

He taught me to distinguish the difference between the many animals that lived in the undergrowth and the quiet steps of a predator. He taught me to leap high, shift in midair, and land in my human form.

Knowing that this was my last session with him, I applied myself more than ever, paying attention and following instructions to a T. I learned everything on the first try and—when it seemed he'd run through everything he'd meant to teach me that day—I asked for more. I even thought I detected a sense of pride in him when I bested him in a leaping exercise in which I cleared a distance of no less than thirty yards.

When we finished and went back into the house, I donned my clothes quickly while he waited for me, his back turned. Despite his unsympathetic and rough treatment, he'd done right by me, and I felt much better prepared to face my life as a werewolf. I knew I still had much more to learn about my wolf and her abilities, as well as the secretive ways of my kind, but I would always be grateful to Eric.

I picked up my duffel bag and slung it over my shoulder. "I won't let the door hit me on my way out," I joked.

"You do that."

I started to climb the stairs to the main floor and had to pause when a strange breeze blew by me. I glanced in every direction, smelling the air, but I only detected Eric's scent. Shrugging it off, I climbed the rest of the steps and had to do a double take when I found Eric reclining on the wall near the exit, picking dirt from his fingernails.

Confused, I glanced the way I'd come, then back at him. "How did you…?"

He smiled without glancing up at me. "It's another perk of being an alpha."

"Teleportation, you mean?"

He scoffed. "Teleportation is science-fiction, Sunder. Not even Midnight Mages can do that. I just move… fast. It's an alpha thing called *fleeting*. Not every alpha can do it, but I think you have the potential."

"You passed me in the hall," I said, realizing that the breeze I'd felt had been Eric. "That was as fast as a vampire."

"Faster," he shrugged one shoulder, "than most at least. The really ancient ones, they might as well be teleporting."

"I had no idea."

"We guard our secrets well, Sunder."

"I'm starting to realize that. Shit, you've been holding out on me, and now that it's our last day, you're rubbing it in."

Eric gave me a crooked smile, loaded with a heavy dose of satisfaction. *The bastard.*

"What else is there?" I asked.

"Wouldn't you like to know?"

I gritted my teeth, my anger bubbling like a witch's brew. "Asshole," I said under my breath and walked past him.

"I'll see you this afternoon," he said, pulling away from the wall.

"Huh?"

"I'll be at Damien's. He told me you'll help him get the

ingredients for his cure."

Damien had called me yesterday to say he would like my help, after all. An unexpected change of heart but a welcomed one.

"We also talked about how well your training is going." Eric went on. "It made us realize that if I teach you a few more things, you might actually be a nice addition to our team. So you're welcome to come back here anytime from now on. Just remember, 4 AM."

My jaw unhinged and nearly dropped to my boobs. Eric Lone, the werewolf with the meanest reputation in all of St. Louis, wanted to keep teaching me out of the goodness of his heart? And join their team? What team? I thought Damien and Eric hated each other.

Eric's blue eyes twinkled, and for the first time, he smiled without sarcasm or conceit. But too quickly, he sobered. "Get the hell out of here before I change my mind."

I backed away toward the door, biting my tongue to hold back a million questions. I wanted to ask all of them at once, but I managed to keep them in. Eric was willing to teach me more, maybe even to move as fast as a vampire.

Holy shit, I kind of felt like I'd won the lottery.

CHAPTER 14

Mom was propped up on a mountain of pillows. The remote control and an e-reader loaded with enough books to last a lifetime rested on her night table. We had brought her home about twenty minutes ago and had made her as comfortable as possible.

Dani came back from the kitchen, carrying a cup of tea, the spoon clinking against the glass as she swirled it around. "Drink this. It will speed up the healing process."

Mom wrinkled her nose. "Is that one of your nasty brews?"

"Nasty or not, don't you want to feel better?"

Staring at the ceiling, Mom pretended to weigh her options, then said, "Hand it here." She took a small sip and made a face. "Gah, what's in it? Bird poop?"

Dani crossed her arms, offering no comment about the tea's ingredients.

"Where has Lucia gotten to?" Mom asked.

"I don't know," I said as I went through Mom's dresser, looking for a nightgown. She wanted to take a shower later and had asked me to find her clean clothes.

A silver baby rattle lay at the bottom of the drawer. I smiled, remembering Lucia playing with it. Apparently, we had all played with it, and before us, my mother and her siblings. I went to pick it up, but as soon as my fingers touched its carved handle, a jolt of electricity seemed to go through me, accompanied by a violent assault to my senses. The sudden sound of many babies crying, the smell of curdled milk, and violent flashes of color nearly knocked me on my butt. I jerked my hand back, stifling a cry, and shook my head, trying to clear it.

What the hell was that?!

I glanced around, but, thankfully, no one had noticed my freak out. I took a few deep breaths and chucked the episode to stress.

Mom reached for her cell phone and started pressing buttons. She made a sound in the back of her throat, then peered up at Dani. "Can you check and see if Lucia is in her bedroom. The Find My Phone app says she's here, but I have my doubts."

A minute later, Dani returned, shaking her head. "She's not there, but her phone is."

"Damn girl!" Mom exclaimed. "I could tell she was itching to go."

"Where?" I asked.

Mom fluffed one of her pillows and rearranged it. "She's made some new friends, and she's been spending a lot of time with them."

"Should we be worried?" Dani asked.

"I don't know yet. That's why I'm trying to keep an eye on her."

Dani glanced my way, then back at Mom. "Let me know if you need me to talk to her."

"Yeah, me too," I said, though I had enough troubles of my

own to add my little sister's to the pile.

I went into the adjacent bathroom and put the clean clothes I'd gathered next to the sink on an empty section of the counter. I considered for a moment, then decided this was as good a time as any to ask my big question, the one that had been burning a hole in my tongue since it perched there.

Mom was fiddling with the remote control when I went back out. Dani was nowhere in sight. When Mom caught me searching for my sister, she set the remote down, leaving the TV on mute as the news rolled by.

"She went to the kitchen to see what to whip up for lunch. You're welcome to stay."

I sat at the foot of the bed. "I can't. I'd love to, but I have to get back to the office. You'll be in great hands, though. No one can take better care of you than Dani."

"That is true. Her teas are nasty, but they do the trick."

"Mom..." Her brown eyes met mine, and her expression grew concerned as she noticed the weight that the single word had carried. "I have something to ask you."

She deflated against her pillows, almost disappearing in their folds. I had no doubt she already knew what I wanted to ask, and judging by her reaction, she had no desire to answer.

I took a deep breath. "Who is he?"

Mom closed her eyes as if she could hide from me.

"You've kept enough secrets from me already," I said. "I hope it isn't your intention to keep more."

I could feel my anger simmering as I prepared for her refusal to confess who my real father was. My hand slowly curled into a fist, resting on my thigh as the seconds ticked by without an answer. But, after a long minute, she spoke and surprised me with her words.

"You're right, Antonietta. I kept you in the dark for too long, and I would have probably continued to do so if no obstacles had gotten in the way. I would have spared you what you must be going through."

A few days ago, I would have agreed that the lies were the best option, but now, everything felt so right, so perfectly aligned, that I couldn't imagine not knowing, not being who I'd become.

"And if I could," she went on, "I would spare you the knowledge of your real father's identity, but I know it wouldn't be right, even if the knowledge might bring you more pain." She paused, looking deep into my eyes as if trying to reach into my soul to make me understand I should leave this topic alone.

But I didn't waver. I'd had enough surprises already, and *this*, I wanted to learn on my own terms.

Mom sighed. "I would also like for you to tell me everything. How life has changed for you, how you're dealing with… the changes. You seem to be doing all right, but you've always been proud and prefer dealing with things on your own."

"It was rough for a bit, but Damien found someone to help me."

"Damien?" she asked, surprised.

"I figured he owed me, so…" I shrugged. "Don't worry, Mom. I'm fine, and I'll tell you anything you want to know, but first…"

"First, you want to know your father's name," she finished for me, looking resigned.

"I do."

"Are you going to try to see him?"

"I don't know. All I know is that I'm ready to find out." I paused. "Why did you lie? Why not tell Dad? I think he would've forgiven you."

"I considered it long and hard, but in the end, I realized what an idiot I had been for cheating on him. He was the same amazing man I'd married. I was the one who'd failed him. He didn't deserve the hurt the truth would have caused him. It wasn't easy to keep up the lie, and the burden served as payment for my mistake. But I think it preserved our family. Our happiness was untouched by my mistakes."

I wanted to say that I was the one paying for her mistakes now, that she had only delayed the hurt, but I wasn't here to fight. Besides, I would take any amount of pain if Dad could be spared.

"I know I have no right to ask anything of you," Mom continued, "but maybe it would be best if you stay away from him. He has changed a lot since we…" She lowered her head unable to finish. Her hands rested on her lap, fidgeting.

"How do you know that?"

"He's an alpha, the leader of a prominent family. His name is often on the news, and not necessarily for good reasons."

I felt the color drain from my face as a list of well-known werewolves flashed before my eyes. I winced as the name "Ulfen Erickson" rose to the very top. I swallowed thickly, waiting for her lips to shape the syllables that would give me all the reasons not to ever approach the man. Except, Mom surprised me with a different name.

"Your father is Travis Hillworth."

CHAPTER 15

The knowledge of my father's identity settled down in my gut like a heavy boulder. I had heard the name Travis Hillworth plenty of times, and like Mom had said, it was rarely in a good light, the more I thought about it even Ulfen Erickson sounded better than him.

I left Mom's house in a daze. Once inside my car by the curb, I surfed the web on my phone, looking at pictures of the man and his family. He was tall, about 6'4". He had dark brown hair and eyes. He wore horn-rimmed glasses and sweaters, which he actually managed to pull off. His face was long and his aquiline nose crooked. He was married and had a daughter and a son—my half-sister and half-brother. That idea gave me all kinds of nausea. I had more siblings, both older than me, which meant he had stepped out on his wife with my mother. What in the world had possessed him to do that? And how had my mother gotten pregnant when that was a rare occurrence between werewolves and non-werewolves?

Could it have been that thing Jake mentioned? What had he

called it? Cravedark?

As I drove back to the office, I struggled with the concept of my mom cheating on Dad with a werewolf. It made absolutely no sense and seemed entirely out of character. Mom had loved Dad, and they had been happy together. When he died, she was devastated because she'd lost the love of her life. If that was how she'd felt about him, then why the hell had she cheated on him?

There was so much more that Mom and I needed to discuss, so many questions that needed answers, but life was moving at breakneck speed, and this would have to wait.

Once at the office, I waited for Rosalina to arrive. She was uncharacteristically late and seemed flustered when she finally got here.

We got a little bit of work done, making phone calls and rearranging appointments and plans. She understood that the priority was helping Damien find a cure so we could save Josh, but I could tell that putting things on hold stressed her out. We had enough money to cover our upcoming loan payment and other bills, but our salaries would take a hit, and after that, we would have to dip into our savings account, which we'd barely started to build. One month and it would be drained completely, negating all our efforts.

Crap! Dani had been right. I shouldn't have signed my name on the dotted line for a condo—not without first building a comfortable financial cushion. If only I were as sensible as my older sister.

After a quick lunch from the pizzeria across the street, we headed out to Damien's place. As I was locking the door to our office, my senses spiked with awareness, freezing me on the spot.

"What's the matter?" Rosalina asked.

"I don't know." I turned the key and glanced around, trying to see what might have caused my sudden alertness, but the street was unusually empty, with only a couple of guys walking on the opposite sidewalk headed for Cup o' Java.

I shook my head. "I guess it's nothing. My senses have been a bit hyperactive. I think my wolf is still settling in."

"Whatever spell Damien put on you, it must've been a humdinger."

We were walking toward my Camaro when the rumble of an engine came around the corner. I immediately recognized it as Jake's Harley. I glanced in the direction of the sound, and as I laid eyes on him, my hypersensitive senses settled down, going back to a comfortable level.

What the hell?

"Was he the reason you were acting so weird?" Rosalina asked, putting two and two together.

"I think so."

"Like you knew he was coming? Like you have spidey sense?"

"I really didn't know he was near, but maybe I should have. Let's get out of here." I didn't want to talk to Jake. It was too hard to be around him. Plus, we had somewhere to be.

Unfortunately, he caught sight of us before we made it to the car and sped his bike in our direction. Damn, if only Eric had taught me how to teleport already. Jake came to a stop, kicked out the stand, got off, and strolled resolutely toward us.

"It was him," he said between clenched teeth. "The other wolf at the warehouse, it *was* Stephen. You were right." He halted in front of me, and I could feel his anger rippling from his body like an energy field. "The fucking bastard. I should kill him."

My eyes darted all around, worried someone might hear him. "Calm down, and don't do anything stupid."

"How are you so sure?" Rosalina asked.

"I called Kaden, our friend in New Orleans. He sent me this picture." He pulled out his phone and retrieved the photograph of a snarling wolf standing on top of an unmade bed, a woman wrapped in the sheets like a burrito, looking terrified. The wolf had reddish fur and glowing blue eyes. It was of medium size, only slightly bigger than Eric's wolf.

"Kaden snapped this picture during a drunken party they had," Jake explained. "They were wasted on this drug called *grim shaggy* or some crap like that, and Stephen decided to shift and scare all the women at the party. He thought it was funny."

That sounded like something College Stephen would've done. Supposedly, he'd been a party animal then, but when I'd met him, all of his friends seemed to think he was reformed. But maybe he hadn't been. Maybe, it had all been a front for his father's sake.

Jake put away his phone, his fists clenching and unclenching as he worked through his anger and disappointment.

"I'm sorry," I said, realizing that this discovery pained him.

He had considered Stephen his friend. When Stephen had gone missing, Jake had moved heaven and earth to find him, had even convinced me to help, pushing aside his personal goal of staying away from me. And arguably, Jake's life had taken a turn for the worse since then, much like mine. Maybe we both had Stephen to blame for our current misery, and for the shithole St. Louis was turning into.

Witchlights! Did Stephen really want a war? Or was he only rebelling against Ulfen?

"How were we so wrong about his character?" I asked. "He must be rotten to the core."

"I can't believe I wasted my time worrying about him," Jake said, his nostrils flaring as anger continued to ripple through him. "I thought I was saving him, and all along I was helping his twisted scheme. I even dragged you into all of this. Toni, I'm sorry."

"It's not your fault," Rosalina said. "You were just trying to do good."

Jake shook his head. "I should have seen through him."

"He fooled all of us," I said. "Rosalina's right. It isn't your fault."

"We have to stop him," he said, taking a deep breath as his disappointment turned to resolve. "The influx of rhabo into the city hasn't let up and more vampires are dying every day. Bernadetta Fiore has summoned her generals. They are gearing up for a war against us."

"How do you know?" I asked.

"All the pack leaders have been communicating, my grandfather included. Their scouts brought reports that say a war is imminent."

"Shit, this is bad." A rush of adrenaline flooded my body as if I were in a fight or flight situation and not simply standing on the sidewalk.

"Um," Rosalina checked the time on her phone. "I'm sorry to interrupt, but we're going to be late, Toni."

I pondered for a moment, then made a decision on the spot. I had no idea if Damien and Eric would get mad at me, but the information Jake had could be useful.

"Why don't you come with us?" I said.

"Where?"

"We're meeting with Damien Ward and Eric Cross. Damien is working on a cure that will cancel rhabo's effects. I also think they're on our side and can help us."

CHAPTER 16

"Who is this?" Damien demanded, giving Jake the once over.

We stood outside his door while he barred the entry, standing like Zorro with fists on hips and his long black cloak hanging from his neck. The only thing spoiling the effect was his top hat. He needed to exchange it for a mask.

"This is Jacob Knight," I said. "He's a… friend of mine. You must remember him from the day you blew a hole in my office."

Damien's left eye twitched. "I'm sorry, but I'm afraid you'll need to leave."

"But I thought we were—" I started to protest.

"No." Damien cut me off. "Change of plans."

He started to close the door, but I blocked it with my foot. "Is Eric here?"

Damien lifted a hand toward my foot, magic crackling between his fingers.

"I'm here," Eric called from within the house. "Let them in, Damien. Quit being so paranoid."

"Paranoid? It's not child's play we're dealing with here."

Eric appeared behind Damien, his blue gaze locking with Jake's silver one. "I'll vouch for him."

"You know him?" the mage asked.

"I know *of* him."

Damien huffed. "That's not good enough."

"He got confirmation for me, Damien," I said. "I was right, Stephen Erickson is behind all of this. Jake fought with me and helped stop that huge shipment of rhabo from flooding the city."

Eric put a hand on Damien's shoulder. "We need all the help we can get. What we're setting out to do is no easy task."

The mage threw his hands up in the air. "Okay, but no more surprises." He whirled and pushed past Eric, his cloak fluttering behind him as he stomped away.

"What a prima donna," Jake said under his breath as we entered.

"I heard that," Damien growled as he disappeared through a door I hadn't noticed before. It was set under the grand staircase, its surface painted to match the wall, so when closed, it would blend in perfectly.

"He's in a bad mood," I pointed out.

"You would be too if your daughter were dying," Eric said.

"What?! His daughter?" Rosalina exclaimed.

"Yeah, he didn't tell you? His daughter is a vampire and is addicted to rhabo."

"No, he didn't mention that," I said, feeling horrible and finally understanding Damien's fury and frustration when he discovered that Jenson and Blake had destroyed his potions room.

"He has a daughter," Rosalina repeated to herself, looking a little bewildered.

"Yes," Eric said. "It may not look like it, but Damien has been around for some time. He was married once."

I blinked at Eric. For someone who was especially secretive about his own personal life, he certainly was being forthcoming about Damien's.

Rosalina frowned, taken aback by all this information. She liked Damien, but maybe learning the more personal tidbits about someone who'd been alive for who knew how long would make her interest in him die down. A person that old would have a lot of baggage. I'd only been around twenty years and look what a clusterbumble my life was.

Jake extended a hand toward Eric. "It's nice to officially meet you."

Eric shook it. "Same here."

Suddenly, the strong scent of aggression filled the air, making my skin prickle. Their interlaced hands squeezed as if to break bone. Keeping eye contact, they took each other's measure, and though Jake towered over Eric by four inches, the smaller man appeared just as intimidating. They held on for a bit too long, making their handshake super awkward.

Rosalina shuffled from foot to foot and threw a nervous glance my way.

My hackles rose, and I felt oddly torn between Jake and Eric, wondering whose side I would be on if they decided to fight. But just as I thought they would shift and size up their wolves or dicks, they broke the handshake and inclined their heads respectfully.

"I don't have all day," Damien's voice echoed through the house as if on speaker phone. Rosalina and I glanced all about, wondering where it was coming from, but it was probably magic.

"We better get down there." Eric went through the false door, gesturing with his hand for us to follow.

Rosalina went first. I followed, Jake at my side.

"What the hell was that?" I asked Jake.

"A moratorium."

"A what?"

"Moratorium. It's when two alpha's agree to commune peacefully and promise not to try to overpower each other."

"Interesting."

Man, I had so much to learn. Would I ever catch up?

From the door, a set of steps led toward a gloomy basement. The area appeared old, unlike the rest of the house, which seemed to have been remodeled recently. The walls were exposed brick with mortar that looked crumbly in places. A dank scent rode the air, reminding me that despite appearances, this place had been built well over a hundred years ago. I wondered if Damien was the original owner.

The mage was waiting for us in a large, semi-lit area. The edges of the room were dipped in shadows, the warm glow of candles unable to reach far enough to let me determine the true dimensions of the space. Some of the furniture I'd seen in the potions room upstairs was now here. Several long worktables and the large armoire with the carved doors and metal handles. Several empty shelves lined one wall, all in need of ingredients to make this place worthy of any mage's proper potions room.

Damien stood behind one of the long worktables. As we approached, he narrowed his eyes at Jake, still distrusting him.

"He's all right, Damien," Eric said. "We communed and have an understanding."

The mage removed his top hat and set it on the table. His white hair lay flat against his scalp, making him look in terrible need of a comb. "Forgive me if I'm not too impressed by agreements between alphas."

Eric made a sound in the back of his throat but said nothing.

"Thanks for letting us help," I said.

Damien forced a smile that didn't reach his eyes. "You have suddenly become… useful," he said.

I frowned, unsure of what he meant.

The mage removed his cloak and set it next to the hat.

His mouth twisted in a smirk. Jake glanced at me, silver eyes twinkling with amusement. He was probably thinking that his prima donna assessment of the mage was right on point.

"Eric tells me you know Kalyll Adanorin, the Seelie Fae Prince." Damien raised his eyebrows, inviting an explanation.

Except I was the one who needed one. How the hell did Eric know I'd met the Prince? I'd never told him. We had never talked about Kalyll. I turned and faced my busybody teacher.

"Who told you that?" I demanded.

"You did." He tapped his temple.

"You mean you *saw* that in my mind?"

He nodded.

"That's just wrong!" It was a flagrant invasion of my privacy,

"You were unguarded the first few times you shifted during our training. It's yet another perk of being an alpha."

"No shit!" I exclaimed. "Does it ever end? I hate all the surprises and not being able to stop any of it. Maybe you need to make me a list of all the alpha perks and teach me more."

"Teach you more?" Jake echoed. "What do you mean?"

Oops! That was the wrong thing to mention.

"And when did you meet the Fae Prince?"

Double whammy!

"Yes," Eric said. "Toni is my student. I'm teaching her the ways of the werewolves."

Jake inhaled deeply, looking as if he wanted to say something, but surprisingly, he held back. Maybe it was that moratorium thing they'd done. Hmm, I really had to learn about that. It would be nice not to argue with Jake at every turn.

"At any rate," Damien said, sounding irritated, "we need you to go to Elf-hame and talk to Prince Kalyll. The Seelie royal family is rumored to have Bitterthorn in their palace stores."

"Bitterthorn?" I asked.

The mage nodded. "It's one of the ingredients I need to formulate the cure."

"You guys are crazy," I said. "I barely know the Prince, and he certainly won't rush into the Seelie *royal* stores to get me this Bitterthorn."

"You said you wanted to help," Damien spoke very slowly as if I was dumber than a brick wall, "and this is the task we have for you."

"I wouldn't even know where to find him," I said. "I doubt he even remembers me."

"Either way," Eric said, "you have to at least try, if you want to save your friend."

I exchanged a hopeless look with Rosalina. Going to Elf-hame to find Kalyll sounded like a big waste of time. I only had access to a small trading post in the outskirts of the Fae realm, so unless the Prince happened to be there by some sort of miracle, I might as well embark on a chase for wild, tutu-wearing geese.

But maybe… I glanced around, one eyebrow raised. "Do either of you have access to anything other than a trading post, because that's all *I* have."

"Well, of course." Damien rolled his eyes. "You don't think we expected you to find him at some stinking trade market. I have passage into the Seelie capital with room for one guest, so you and I will go together."

"You're kidding," I said in a whisper.

"No, I'm not. I would like us to leave right away. There's no time to waste."

Holy witchlights. I was going to Elyndell.

CHAPTER 17

"I don't like this," Jake said, pulling me aside as Eric and Damien conferred in the opposite corner of the room. "I don't like that mage and messing with the Fae rarely comes to any good."

I pulled my hand from his grip. "I'm doing this, Jake, and there's nothing you can do or say to stop me."

Narrowing my eyes, I expected him to argue, but he simply lowered his head and gave me a single nod. I looked him up and down, wondering if he was feeling all right. Maybe he'd caught a bug, and it'd gone to his head. Telling me what to do and insisting on it when I refused was his favorite pastime.

"I wish you wouldn't, but it's your decision," he said.

I was about to touch his forehead to check for a spike in his temperature when Rosalina sidled closer. "How long do you think you'll be gone?"

"I've no idea." I had never been to Elyndell and had absolutely no clue how to find Prince Kalyll.

Rosalina frowned, looking as if she was going to be sick to her stomach. Had she caught the same bug Jake had?

"What is it?" I asked.

She shook her head. "Nothing, just me worrying about *everything*, but the most important thing is that you get back safely."

And by *everything*, I was pretty sure she meant the agency. Was I making the right decision? We had discussed it and agreed that we had to help Josh and Aaron, but was she having second thoughts?

Jake's clear eyes darted back and forth between Rosalina and me, his interest piqued by our conversation. Giving him a dirty glare, I pulled Rosalina aside.

"Are you sure you're okay with us doing this?" I asked. "Are you getting cold feet?"

"No. Not when I think of poor Josh, and how lost Aaron looked when we told him. I wouldn't be able to live with myself if we don't help them. We can't sacrifice our integrity for monetary gain."

It was more than just money, though. It was our dream, what we'd been working so hard to accomplish. We didn't want more than most people—just a way to be independent and feel accomplished. But if our business failed, we wouldn't starve. Worst case scenario, she might have to go back to being a barista while I rejoined the homeless, but we would be alive. Unlike Josh.

"Okay," I said. "We both have to be on the same page. I couldn't do any of this if you didn't agree. We're partners." I wanted to make sure she understood that. There could be no regrets later, no matter the outcome.

"Are you ready?" Damien approached, followed by Eric.

"As ready as I'll ever be," I said.

He extended a large purse in my direction. It looked like something an old grandma might carry around. It was the size of a backpack, made of black velvet with a pattern of golden flowers. It had a silken drawstring, and bright yellow lining.

I took the bag with hesitation for fear it might zap my senses like the rattle had done. It didn't. "What is this?"

"Our supplies," Damien said. "Food and the like. We can't eat anything the Fae might offer us—not in Elyndell, anyway."

I glowered at him. What did he think I was? His pack mule? I set the bag on the worktable, and just as I was about to release it, the strong scent of mothballs hit me, followed by what sounded like a klaxon blaring in my ear. A rainbow of color flashed before my eyes. I recoiled, blinking. *Really? Again?!* What was going on? These episodes felt too much like when I went into a trance. Were my powers changing? It certainly seemed so. What more would I manage to see if I held on to the bag? I needed to talk to Damien about this new development, but right now wasn't a good time.

"I'm not carrying that ugly thing," I said, faking a shiver to disguise my reaction.

"Ugly?!" Damien exclaimed. "It belonged to my mother."

"No wonder. She could probably be my Nonna's Nonna." If I had to guess, the woman had probably been born in the early 1900s, maybe even earlier, which beat Nonna by about fifty years.

The mage pointed a finger at my face. "I'll have you know that—"

"Damien," Eric interrupted, "I'm sure *you* can carry the bag." There was something in his blue eyes that seemed to tell him not to push his luck with me. Damien grumbled something under his breath but picked up the bag.

I smirked.

The mage went for his cloak, and with dexterous fingers, tied it around his neck. Next, he set the silken top hat on his head. He cast a furtive glance in Rosalina's direction. So far, he had acted as if she wasn't there, but clearly, he was quite aware of her presence.

"Good luck, Damien," Rosalina said, realizing he wasn't as ambivalent as he would have her believe.

"Thank you," he blurted out. Tearing his copper gaze away from my friend, he squared his shoulders. "Let's go."

I started toward the steps, taking the lead out of the basement.

"Where are you going?" The mage asked.

"Hmm, to wherever your entry point into Elf-hame is." Mine was in Tower Grove Park. I had to sit in the Turkish Pavilion and trace my assigned rune into one of the tables, and a second later, I was in Pharowyn.

"My entry point is wherever I want it to be," Damien said, holding up a smooth wooden carving in the shape of a coin. It was about the size of a silver dollar with minute designs I had no time to decipher. He put the charm in his pocket and crooked his elbow, inviting me to take it.

"Really? No fair." I threaded my arm through his, wishing I had a pass that let me access Elf-hame from wherever I was. "You're going to have to tell me what to do to get this type of access."

"*Pshaw*, they don't give this to just anyone."

I glared at him. *Arrogant bastard!* If it weren't because I needed him to craft this cure, I would sit on his stupid top hat.

"We'll contact you when we get back," Damien said to Eric, then turning to me, he added, "see you on the other side."

The last thing I saw were Jake's worried eyes.

ജ്ജ

The world washed away. The color on the walls that surrounded me ran down like paint on a canvas, melting to a puddle on the floor. Only darkness was left behind, reminding me of that place I visited whenever I was in a trance.

I clung to Damien, fearful to get separated and lost in the vast nothingness. As if a reel were running backward, all the color that had puddled under our feet started climbing up again, streaks of blue, red, and yellow rising and weaving themselves into a new backdrop, quickly forming shapes that I gradually recognized.

Massive trees the size of skyscrapers. Distant mountains capped with snow. Clouds as fluffy as cotton balls, and a blue sky several shades darker than any I'd ever seen. A prairie stretched before us, dotted with flowers of all colors and shapes. I blinked at the splendor, feeling as if I'd landed in some sort of impressionist painting. The colors were vivid, and I had no name for most of their shades.

"It's… it's gorgeous," I said, sounding out of breath.

"I suppose," Damien shrugged, "but we're not here to admire the scenery." He turned, forcing me to face in the opposite direction and shaking my arm off as if I were an unwanted attachment.

The sight that greeted me on the other side left me even more speechless than the one at my back. A magical city sprawled before me. It was a place apt for fantastic fairy tales with princesses and queens, and dragons and unicorns.

Elyndell was vast and blended perfectly with the surrounding scenery. Earth-toned buildings grew around trees, over hills, and along riverbanks. Mossy paths meandered between the structures, running in no particular order and making me wonder if the roads and structures had actually grown instead of been built.

At the center of it all, a white tower rose, vines crawling up its sides and getting lost into its many windows. The city seemed to grow away from the tower, expanding in every direction as far as the eye could see. The place was as big as any city in my realm, except without the noise of engines and their pollutants.

"What is that?" I asked, pointing at the tower.

"The Vine Tower. It's where the royal family lives."

My eyes grew wider as I tried to imagine the inside of the structure.

"If you're done gawking…" Damien said and began walking towards the closest moss-covered path.

I stumbled after him, not done gawking at all. Everything I saw drew my eye. Twisted trees, their branches getting lost inside the walls or windows of small, picturesque cottages. Swings made of vines. Gurgling fountains that seemed to rise from the ground. Beautiful Fae males and females, but most surprising of all: Fae children. I had never seen their young before, and if the grown specimens were beautiful, their miniature versions were lovely little cherubs fallen from the heavens, their huge eyes and smooth skin an artist's dream.

After a short walk during which I gawked at everyone, and everyone blatantly ignored us as if we were invisible—clearly, they didn't want us here—Damien ushered me into what appeared to be some sort of tavern. The place was built from millions of tiny branches all stuck together. Windows in the shapes of honeycombs ran in a line all around the structure. Inside, it was as bright as daylight. I blinked up and realized there was no roof over our heads and the floor was nothing but thick grass, kept short. A tree as wide as a house stood back and center. Its sprawling roots growing from the ground to create chairs and tables where an array of Fae folk sat eating from wooden bowls and drinking from ceramic tankards.

Damien approached a counter that was also made from tree roots, its surface polished to a perfect sheen. A female stood behind the counter. She had luscious red hair and turquoise eyes that slanted at a forty-five degree angle. Her ears protruded, ending in a sharp point about three inches away from her head. A snake that looked more like a dragon curled around her neck, tasting the air with its forked tongue.

At first, she acted like we weren't there, but her demeanor changed completely when Damien spoke.

"*Ven konodin*, dear madam," Damien said, inclining his head.

The female didn't quite smile, but sharp canine teeth flashed as she inclined her head. "May I be of assistance," she asked in a thick, lilting accent.

"You may, I am looking for Rosia Wynthas, do you know where I may find him?"

"Apologies, I don't know the individual you speak of." She flashed her teeth again. "I would ask if you wish to drink or eat something, but I have a feeling you won't accept." Her turquoise eyes twinkle with malice.

I scratched my neck, taking a deep breath and willing my wolf to calm down.

The female's gaze snapped in my direction. "A shifter," she said. "Your kind isn't welcome here. Please, leave."

At the hostile comment, my wolf was ready to pick a fight, but gratefully, she now listened to reason. This was no time to act tough.

"No problem," I said. "I'll wait outside."

I turned to leave and started toward the door when it suddenly burst open and what looked like a chubby child stomped inside. On second look, the thick braided beard draping over an expansive belly made me wonder if the Fae also had ugly children. But when he spoke with a voice like rumbling rocks grinding together, all lingering doubts went out the window. The short male was not a child at all. He wore a thickly weaved tunic and bulky boots lined in fur. He had a bulbous nose and beady eyes.

The knocking of wooden utensils and the gentle chatter that had filled the tavern ceased completely.

"White Damien," the newcomer boomed. "I didn't want to believe my ears when they heard you were here, but I guess you are as unwise as you are cocky."

Damien winced and slowly turned to face the newcomer. "*Ven konodin*, Glimlock," Damien said, his grimace quickly morphing into a smug grin as he faced the smaller male.

"*Ven konodin*, my arse," Glimlock said, then in one swift motion he pulled out a short sword from the scabbard at his back, murder spelled on his weather-beaten features.

The mage sighed as if the little male were nothing more than a first grader brandishing a crayon. For my part, I took several steps back until I hit the wall. Whatever this was, I wanted no part of it. Only the witchlights knew what had happened between these two. Though something told me the Fae wasn't the one to blame.

Glimlock twirled his sword, then pointed it at Damien's middle and lunged. I held my breath as the mage stood impassively and, in the last possible instant, put a hand up. Abruptly, his attacker came to a stop as if someone were holding him back by his tunic.

Leaning forward and stretching his arm as much as he could, Glimlock sliced his sword left and right trying to reach Damien, but he was a few inches too far.

"Fight, you coward," Glimlock rumbled, his booted feet sliding on the grass as he seemed to run in place, desperate to reach his target. The sight was comical and sad at the same time.

The mage crossed his arms and regarded him down an upturned nose. A few of the patrons looked on with angry frowns, but others snickered. Neither did anything to intervene.

"Are you quite done?" Damien asked in a bored tone.

To my surprise, I found myself growing irritated at the mage.

The little guy was exhausting himself, running in place and brandishing his sword like a lunatic, hopelessly wasting his energy, while Damien acted like a complete asshole.

"Hey, cut it out," I found myself saying.

The mage glanced in my direction and seemed surprised to find that I was staring straight at him and not at his would-be attacker.

"Excuse me?" he spat, looking annoyed. "*I* need to cut it out?"

I walked over and put my hands on my hips. "Yeah, you! Leave him alone."

"Seriously?"

Glimlock stopped his treadmill workout and blinked up at me. "I can fight my own battles," he rumbled at me.

"I don't doubt that, dear sir," I said. "But this mage isn't fighting fair. In fact, he isn't fighting at all."

"Stay out of this," Damien scoffed. "This belligerent garden gnome has been harassing me ever since our paths crossed. He is a nuisance and a pest."

"I'll have to agree with that," the female behind the counter said as she buffed the already-clean counter with a piece of cloth.

"I am not a garden gnome," Glimlock spat, resuming his useless attempts to stab Damien. "I put a curse on you and all your descendants, White Damien."

"Whatever you did to him," I said, "just apologize. We're wasting our time."

Damien frowned. "Whatever *I* did to *him*?"

"Yeah, something tells me you're to blame."

"I didn't do anything to him. It was all a big misunderstanding."

Glimlock stopped and put down his sword again, looking exhausted. "That was no misunderstanding. My wife left me because of you."

Huh?! I didn't see that coming.

A small gasp went through the crowd. They had abandoned their food and turned their attention to us. It seemed that, without television, this was as close to a soap opera as they would ever get.

"I had nothing to do with that," Damien protested.

"You gave her a black chrysanthemum," Glimlock said as if that explained everything.

Damien rubbed his forehead. "I have tried to explain that I didn't know the significance of what I was doing. I was just trying to be nice to her."

"I was just trying to be nice to her," Glimlock mimicked in a nasally voice. "Any idiot knows that black chrysanthemums give females the wandering eye."

Did they? Was that a thing everywhere? Or only here in Elfhame? Hmm, I was starting to see that it might have really been a misunderstanding, a clash of cultures most likely.

"The first strapping chap she saw," Glimlock went on, "she was off, chasing him. Now she lives across the way with my neighbor, raising his chickens and his crops, while mine go unattended."

Well, if that was the only reason why he wanted a wife, maybe she was better off without him.

"I miss her so much." Glimlock started crying, large tears spilling onto his rosy cheeks and getting lost in his thick beard. A snot bubble popped out of one nostril as he blubbered.

Oh, dear!

Damien shot daggers at me, clearly blaming me for the mushy display.

"But, you're sorry about it, aren't you, *White Damien*?" I said in a helpful tone.

The mage shook his head ever so slightly. "Yes, I'm quite sorry."

"Sorry will not bring my Ennora back," Glimlock blubbered.

What a hopeless situation. For a moment, I didn't know what else to do, then an idea occurred to me.

"Um, Glimlock, what if… you gave your wife another black chrysanthemum, and then you strut about to make sure she sees you first."

"If it were that easy, I would have already won her back, but black chrysanthemums are near impossible to find. I honestly don't know where this idiot got one and took it upon himself to ruin my life."

I turned to Damien. "Where did you get it?"

He raised one white eyebrow, then addressed Glimlock. "If I promised to get one for you, will you leave me alone?"

Glimlock swatted tears from his eyes. "Can you do that?"

Damien opened his mouth to answer, but paused, casting a glance about the room. Several males were listening in rapt attention. The mage leaned down toward Glimlock and whispered in a barely audible tone.

"I can but with one condition."

"You have no right to set conditions, you dishonorable human."

"Shh," Damien pressed a finger to his lips. "Do you want your wife back or not?"

Glimlock huffed and thought for a long moment. Finally, he said, "Right then, what condition?"

"Let's get out of here and make a deal."

CHAPTER 18

A little creek of turquoise water skimming with white foam gurgled in front of us. Fish of gold, silver, and blue swam about, hiding in between reeds and smooth stones. The perfume of flowers rode the fresh air, making me realize how unclean the air in our realm was.

We sat on a conglomeration of large boulders next to the creek. Glimlock had not sheathed his sword, and I doubted Damien had removed his defensive spell.

The Fae scanned me up and down. "That's some funny garments you wear. What are those?" He pointed at my tennis shoes.

"Those are my kicks," I said. "They're pretty comfy." I wiggled my toes.

The Fae appeared skeptical. He sneaked a stubby finger through his beard, scratched his chin, and shifted his attention to Damien. "Speak up, then, what is your condition?"

"You deliver goods to the Vine Tower, do you not?" Damien asked.

"Aye, but what is it to you?"

"We would like to speak to Prince Kalyll," Damien said. "It's a matter of life or death."

Glimlock huffed. "If you think I will help you get into the Vine Tower, you're right mad."

"We don't need to get into the tower," I interrupted, sensing that Glimlock would not concede any ground in this matter.

Damien glared, his expression seeming to say "what the hell are you doing?"

"I know Prince Kalyll," I said. "I would just like a moment to talk to him. Maybe, instead, you could tell me where I can find him."

"If you know him," Glimlock raised a bushy eyebrow, "request a hearing, like everybody else."

"That would take an inordinate amount of time, which we don't have," Damien said. "Foreigners always fall to the back of the line and are invariably told to come back the next day, at which point they're ushered to the back of an entirely new line."

"As it should be," Glimlock said with a firm nod.

"Please, Glimlock," I begged. "If you can help us in any way, we would be eternally grateful to you."

The Fae pushed away from the boulder and, standing right at eye level, peered at me. "*Please?*" he repeated. "That's a word I've never heard from a human's lips."

"Really?" I blinked in surprise. "That's unfortunate. How many of us have you met?"

"Just the one." He pointed at Damien.

"Oh, well, that explains it." I wrinkled my nose at Damien. "You're giving us all a bad name."

"I may know where Prince Adanorin is," Glimlock said after a moment of contemplation.

I perked up. "You do?"

He gave one decisive nod. "But first," he put out a hand, "my chrysanthemum."

Damien didn't move and continued to sit with his arms folded across his chest. "Can we trust him?"

"Give it a rest, Damien," I blurted out, anger getting the best of me. "I'd say he's more trustworthy than you." I turned to the Fae. "Please, Glimlock, don't go by *White Damien* to judge us all. It would be like judging all birds because you've met a chicken."

"How dare you?!" Damien exclaimed. "In me, he has met an eagle. The rest of you are the chickens."

I rolled my eyes.

Glimlock sputtered a laugh. "What a sorry eagle," he managed, then kept laughing, a hand pressed to his ample belly. His laugh was so hearty and infectious that I couldn't help but join him.

Damien threw his arms up in the air. "Enough of this nonsense." He twirled his hands and a black chrysanthemum appeared between his fingers.

Glimlock's laugh froze midway, and his beady eyes opened as wide as golf balls, nearly popping out of his head. He snatched the flower away from Damien and cradled it near his chest as if it were a delicate baby.

"Oh, Ennora, I shall hold you in my arms tonight." Tears glittered in the corner of his eyes, and I felt genuinely happy for him.

"Now," Damien said, "where can we find Prince Kalyll?"

Glimlock explained carefully as Damien and I did our best to memorize his directions. As we departed on our way, the Fae placed a fist on his chest.

"Young shifter," Glimlock inclined his head. "I must say, you have done a great deal to change my opinion of your kind.

Farewell."

ꙮ

An hour later, Damien and I were still riding atop the two dappled ponies Glimlock had let us borrow—for a few gold coins, mind you. Damien had reluctantly pulled the gold out of his granny bag and had promised the Fae to return the beasts.

"If your directions don't lead us directly to the Prince," the mage had warned, "I'll come back and give your Ennora back to your neighbor."

"Don't listen to him," I'd said, glowering at Damien. "He won't do such a thing."

We were now on the eastern road out of Elyndell as Glimlock had instructed, and every time I glanced in Damien's direction, I had to stifle a laugh. He looked comical on the pony, his long legs nearly touching the ground, his cloak tented over the animal's rump.

"These aren't exactly ponies, are they?" I asked, trying to make conversation. "I mean, they're small but not as small as the ponies I've seen back home."

"There are different pony breeds. These can be ridden by adults. Marginally," he answered coldly. He seemed distracted and not very interested in conversation.

We were supposed to ride about thirty minutes on this road, then another hour heading north where the road forked. The directions weren't exactly making me feel at ease about finding Kalyll. They were too vague and made me wish for the reassuring voice of my GPS telling me to "turn right in twenty yards" or else end up on the wrong side of town.

Every few minutes, Damien shot a little bolt of lightning into the pony's butt, causing the animal to yelp and prance forward until it slowed down and he repeated the process all over again.

I spurred my pony forward to catch up. "Stop zapping the poor horse."

"We don't have all day. I would rather get there and back before nightfall. You don't want to be in these woods when it turns dark."

"Oh, yeah?" I glanced around, wondering what he meant. I didn't know enough about Fae kind and nothing about their realm, so I decided it was best to trust Damien.

After that, I started noticing strange sounds coming from the nearby trees. My eyes darted in their sockets like balls on a pool table. My wolf was on edge, ready to come out at the smallest threat. When my back began to hurt from sitting so stiffly and alert, I tried to start another conversation to distract myself.

"How old is your daughter, Damien?" I asked.

He scratched the side of his neck and took so long to answer that I thought he would ignore my question. At last, he said, "she was thirty-four when she was made into a vampire. Now, she is nearly fifty."

"What's her name?"

"Liliana."

"I'm sorry she's ill, and I really hope I can convince Prince Kalyll to give us the Bitterthorn."

"Me, too. Me, too."

My ass began to hurt like hell one hour into the ride. I shifted in the saddle, wincing at the pain. "I wish I had one of those shifting rings, so I could run in my wolf form," I complained. "It would be a lot more comfortable than this."

I surprised myself with my own words. It was the first time I'd shown favor for four legs over two, and I had a feeling it wouldn't be the last. The more comfortable I got with my wolf, the more I suspected I would enjoy spending time in that shape. It had its advantages for sure, especially in woodsy terrain like this.

"That would be a bad idea," Damien said. "Your wolf stench would make the creatures around us feel threatened, and I can assure you it wouldn't bode well for us."

Creatures around us?

I hadn't seen anything but birds flitting about, but I knew better than to be fooled by appearances when it came to the Fae folk. Any kind of creature could live in these woods. The Fae were as varied in species as humans were varied in their levels of *bullshittery*. I'd heard of sprites, goblins, pucas, kelpies, gnomes, brownies, and more. Only the witchlights knew what else was out there.

I suddenly imagined tiny devils with dinnerware-sized pitchforks raining from the treetops, trying to skewer our eyes out with their weapons. I urged my pony closer to Damien's, hoping he had some sort of magical shield that could keep these devilish creatures away.

"That must be the mound Glimlock gave us as a marker," the mage said, pointing a long finger toward a hill with a lone willow tree on top.

"Yeah, that looks just like what he described."

The path toward the mound was lined with trees. Their branches met above us, allowing only a patchy view of the sky. We were almost there, when the leaves above us rustled, creatures rained from the sky and knocked us from our horses.

I yelped and went sprawling on the ground, landing on my stomach. A heavy weight crashed on top of me. A knife met my neck. I growled, ready to shift as adrenaline flooded every corner of my body. My claws sprang into place.

"Control yourself, Toni," Damien cried out in a strained voice.

"Don't shift or you'll ruin everything."

Gritting my teeth, I turned my head to glare at Damien. He was also on his stomach, face scrunched against the ground and a knife at his throat. A lithe Fae female sat on top of him. She was blond and wore banded armor with a familiar coat of arms painted in the middle. A pair of green feline eyes set into a pale face glared back at me. I strained to glance behind me, but all I could perceive out of the corner of my eye was a tall shape looming over me.

I kicked my legs as my wolf rose within me, ready for a fight.

"Listen to me," Damien said, his copper gaze drilling into mine. "They're royal guards. If we fight them, we'll never get to talk to Prince Kalyll."

Royal guards? How did he know that?

The armor, you idiot.

I'd seen the coat of arms on Kalyll's guards before, hadn't I?

Royal guards. Royal guards. I repeated inside my head over and over, trying to convey the meaning to my wolf. She was ready to go nuclear on these Fae, blind rage consuming her, but she had to listen.

"Take deep breaths," Damien instructed. "You are in control."

I focused on his voice and did as he said. Little by little, I gathered my wits, quietly reasoning with my wolf, gently exerting my command over her.

"Good job," the mage said soothingly as my claws retracted, and I let out a shuddering breath.

"What business do you have with our Prince?" The Fae on top of Damien demanded.

"We wish to speak to him, nothing else," Damien answered.

Gruffly, the guards pulled us to our feet, keeping the knives at our throats.

"Tie them up," the female said.

Royal guards. Royal guards. I chanted again as a reminder to my wolf, who seemed bent on making an appearance.

This is all for Josh and Aaron. Keep it together.

That seemed to do the trick, for now. But if they continued manhandling me, I didn't know how much longer I would manage.

"This one's a shifter, Misra," the guard behind me said in a deep tenor. "Ropes won't hold her."

"Tie her up anyway," Misra responded.

The guard removed the knife from my throat, then jostled my arms up and down as he secured a rope around my wrists. When he was done, he pushed me forward. I stumbled in Damien's direction and finally got a good look at my attacker. To my surprise, he looked a lot like his female companion. Same blond hair. Same green feline eyes.

Misra and her male doppelganger pointed their sharp knives straight toward our hearts.

Taking deep, calming breaths, I stood shoulder to shoulder with Damien, facing the imposing Fae guards, whose matching armor was more impressive than Thor's outfit in *The Avengers* movies. Their blond, long hair also matched the son of Zeus's mane, except it was straight like silken sheets.

"Prince Kalyll has no business with humans," Misra said. "Why are you truly here?"

"We want to ask him for a favor," I said. "I've met the Prince before, and I was hoping he could help me."

The guards exchanged a glance, then laughed. Misra had just opened her mouth to say more, when a terrible screeching sound came from the other side of the mound.

"It has started," the male guards said. "What do we do with these two?"

"Maybe we feed them to the reapgrubs," she responded,

looking pleased with her idea.

"The what?" I asked, glancing sideways at Damien. "What are they talking about?"

"Reapgrubs are a crop plague," Damien said. "They must have an infestation."

Misra took a step closer and pressed her knife to Damien's throat. "Maybe you sent them."

"I did not," the mage answered calmly, despite the sharp weapon next to his jugular. "But I can help you get rid of them."

The guards scoffed. "What can a human do against a swarm of reapgrubs?"

The screeches over the mound grew louder and hectic. They were joined by thumps and screams and curses. Maybe a battle had begun. The guards shifted in place, looking as if they were itching to run over and help.

"I'm not just any type of human," Damien said. "I'm a Copper Mage."

"A mage?" Misra echoed, sounding surprised.

"That is a lie," the male guard said.

"His eyes are strange, Ladresel," Misra pointed out. "I think I've heard that magic disturbs their pupils." She paused, and after some thought said, "Prove it."

Damien smiled, then slowly lifted his hands up in the air. The rope they'd used to bind him now rested limply between his fingers.

"That doesn't prove anything," Ladresel said. "Anyone can do that."

"And how about this?" The mage lowered his hands and offered the guard a hissing cobra, its hood extended, its black, beady eyes shiny and set on the guard.

Ladresel jumped back, his eyes full of terror. "I hate snakes!"

With a quick flick of his wrist, Damien made the snake disappear, leaving nothing behind, not even the rope. "Satisfied?" he asked.

"Maybe he *can* help," Ladresel said.

Misra narrowed her eyes, clearly battling with the decision. She didn't trust us, not one bit.

"They both could have attacked us," Ladresel pondered. "But they didn't."

Misra shrugged. "And what if their target is the Prince."

"He can judge for himself. He would not be afraid of them."

Misra nodded in agreement, then flicked her knife in the direction of the mound. "Walk."

We turned and did as we were told. The guards stayed close behind, their knives at the ready. As we approached, the sounds of battle grew louder. A shrill scream of something like a banshee on its way to hell rent the air. A shiver slid down my back, and it was all I could do not to shift. I bit my lower lip and winced at the pain, but I had to admit that I was doing much better than I would have expected. This was the first time I'd had to use pain to keep my wolf at bay, which was a great improvement from a week ago.

As we rounded the corner, something flew through the air and thudded to the ground right in front of me. I yelped and jumped back, staring at the hideous green gremlin that lay at my feet. The creature was the size of a Chihuahua and had spindly limbs tipped with razor-sharp claws and covered in slimy warts. Its ears were long and floppy, and sharp teeth set in rows filled its mouth. I covered my nose as an awful stench rose from the creature, a mixture of sulfur and garbage rot.

Afraid that the little beast would jump back up even though it appeared as dead as a doorknob, I reluctantly glanced up at the raging melee that spread before us. On a wide farm field, royal guards armed with long swords and shields fought against hundreds, if not thousands, of the green vermin. Attacking like swarming locusts, the reapgrubs pushed on their skinny limbs and soared toward their opponents, claws extended and ready to disfigure whoever stood in their path. As they rained down, the guards sliced with their swords, trying to cut them in half with varying levels of success.

As if that weren't enough, more of the gremlins scuttled over the ground and climbed on the Fae guards as if they were trees. There they found gaps in the guards' armor, and sank in their teeth and claws.

Already many of the little monsters lay on the ground, spewing slimy blood and twitching as they died. But a few of the guards had also fallen, and their bodies now crawled with reapgrubs like lollipops in an ant pile.

In the fray, one warrior stood out. He was massive, taller than all the rest. His blue-black hair whipped through the air along with twin swords as he cut down creature after creature, slicing them to bits as if he were some sort of Ninja blender set on high.

Prince Kalyll looked magnificent in his shining armor, maiming his foes with such skill that none of them managed to lay their scrawny fingers on him.

Despite their efforts, however, the group as a whole wasn't doing so well, and it wouldn't be long before they got overwhelmed by their enemies' sheer numbers.

"Do something, mage!" Misra snarled.

Not waiting to be told twice, Damien took a step forward, eyes narrowed as he assessed the situation. I tensed all over, hoping he had some good trick up his sleeve. After a long moment that made me doubt he could actually help, he crouched next to the dead creature at my feet and stuck his hands into the gaping wound in its belly.

Bile rose up my throat as the reapgrub's awful stench redoubled.

Unfazed, the mage rummaged inside the beast's abdominal cavity as if he were searching for treasure.

"What in the name of Oorus is he doing?" Misra demanded. "He's mad. He's right mad."

When Damien rose to his feet, his hands were dripping with thick slime, and his eyes were glowing an intense red. That was when I noticed his lips were moving at a prodigious speed. Clearly, he was issuing some kind of spell, though I had no idea what kind.

"Maybe we should step back," I said, cautiously retreating from the mage.

The Fae guards seemed reluctant, but when red energy started crackling between Damien's slimy fingers, the two put some distance between themselves and the mage.

As the energy grew brighter around Damien's fingers and started climbing toward his elbows, he pointed his hands toward the sky and released a spider web of thunderbolts. A second later, a clump of clouds gathered above the ongoing battle. They churned with sizzling red energy, promising an electric storm from hell.

Prince Kalyll glanced up as he impaled one of the reapgrubs through the eye. His fierce gaze darted to and fro until he spotted us. His already-determined expression grew sharper, and even from a distance, it managed to intimidate me.

"By the light of Tresta!" Ladresel exclaimed. "That's going to kill everyone."

Arms extended, he lunged in Damien's direction.

"No!" I cried out, trying to stop him, but it was too late.

The guard crashed into Damien, wrapping his arms around the mage's waist. But even as they fell, Damien twirled his wrist toward the clouds and spoke in a commanding voice.

"Decursus incitatus!"

As soon as the words left his lips, red lightning began falling from the sky. Its booms were deafening and echoed through the open field, and its flashing energy blinded us all.

CHAPTER 19

The field turned into a plasma globe as bolts of electricity struck the ground. I clamped my hands over my ears, the hairs on the back of my arms standing on end, and watched in horror as the hell storm raged over the reapgrubs, the royal guards, and Kalyll himself.

Oh, shit! What had Damien done? He had unleashed hell on the Seelie Prince—son of Eithne and Beathan Adanorin. Kalyll was going to fry like a French fry, and we would die in Elf-hame, probably tortured and dismembered by the King and Queen themselves.

I was considering whether to run or face my end when the reapgrubs began dropping to the ground like mosquitoes in a zapper. The red lightning coursed through everyone in the field, including the Prince, but it only affected the creepy devils.

Their hideous bodies twisted and jerked. Their screeches became louder and carried an edge of desperation. They went on convulsing for a long minute while the royal guards stared dumbfounded, cautiously backing away from the agonizing little beasts.

Suddenly, a hush descended over the field, and only the rustling of the crops in the field disturbed the thick silence.

Ladresel rose to his feet, his mouth wide open in surprise, his blond hair swaying about him as he helped Damien to his feet.

The Prince and his guards sheathed their weapons and went around helping their fallen friends, kicking the reapgrubs off their injured bodies.

I sidled next to Damien. "For a moment, I thought you'd gone crazy, but you did it."

He responded with a grunt as he watched the Prince walk around the battlefield, helping make the wounded comfortable, patting shoulders, and saluting with a fist to his heart.

We stayed put at the edge of the field, but every few minutes, the Prince glanced our way as if to make sure we were still there. Ladresel and Misra stayed by us, casting glances in Damien's direction. At last, Prince Kalyll pulled away from his guards and headed our way. His movements were lithe and self-assured. His armor glinted in the sun, making him look like some sort of god. I was struck by his beauty all over again. I had first seen him in Yalgrun's shop a few weeks ago, but his chiseled face was imprinted in my memory.

When he stopped in front of us, Damien inclined his head respectfully. "Prince Kalyll Adanorin, what an honor."

The Prince's cobalt blue gaze drifted from Damien to me, and what he said next left me as speechless as the last time I'd seen him.

"Antonietta Sunder, I find myself confused *and* grateful for your presence here. You and your friend have spared us a difficult if not impossible fight." He placed a hand on his chest and bowed. "I am grateful for your help. May you introduce your companion?"

"Um, uh, y-yes, sure," I babbled. "This is Copper Mage Damien Ward."

Kalyll bowed again toward Damien. "I must repay your help."

The mage and I exchanged a glance. Well, wasn't that convenient? I could only hope that the price of what Damien had done for the Prince matched that of what we'd come to request.

Damien nodded, encouraging me to speak. I frowned at him. He was the one who had saved the day. Maybe he should be the one to do the talking, not me. The mage narrowed his eyes, insistent.

"Prince Kalyll," I said. "There is, indeed, something you could do to help us."

"I will do everything within my power to do so." The Prince turned to Ladresel and Misra. "Make yourselves useful and help the injured."

"Yes, my Prince," they both said in unison, then pounded their chests, and ran off to follow orders.

"You may speak freely, now," Kalyll said.

I nodded once. "I must begin by explaining that we came to Elf-hame in search of you," I said, realizing that I was speaking very formally, like I'd swallowed an English professor.

The Prince raised his eyebrows, but said nothing.

"A farmer who delivers goods to the Vine Tower told us where to find you," I continued, "and we headed this way on borrowed ponies, hoping to find you and gain an audience with you, all on the slim chance that you might remember me."

"I do remember you very well," he said, his eyes glinting. I got the feeling he knew more about me than our chance encounters should have afforded him, but that was unlikely.

"I am glad you do." I inclined my head to express gratitude and relief. "What we wish to request from you is not for us, but for others back in our realm who are ill. You see, Damien needs Bitterthorn to craft a cure to save them from sure death."

"Bitterthorn?" Prince Kalyll said, his deep voice rising a couple of octaves with surprise.

He sounded as incredulous as if I'd just asked him to exchange his armor for a lace bustier right before going into battle against barbed dragons. It took him a moment to sober up. "It is no trifle you ask for, Antonietta Sunder, but on my honor and for the deed you have done for us today, I will listen to you further and, based on your answer, will determine the righteousness of your request."

So, with my heart in my hand and hopes for Aaron and Josh's happiness and Liliana's life, I told Prince Kalyll everything.

ᴥ

The Seelie Prince gave us exactly two Bitterthorn leaves. No more, no less.

Ten hours after we arrived in Elf-hame, we reappeared in Damien's basement. The place was absolutely dark until he snapped his fingers and the candles around the room came to life.

No one was there, and the basement was spooky, but after being in the Fae realm, being back felt good. Safe.

"I will get started working on the cure right away," Damien said, moving around the room, gathering utensils for his work.

"Here?" I said. "Aren't you worried Stephen will send someone to destroy it again?"

"I added additional reinforcements to the house. They'll get a big surprise if they return."

I guessed there was no point in arguing with him. He knew what he was doing better than me. Besides, this was for his daughter, so I knew he would fight to the death to protect her only chance left at life—or death, whichever way vampires saw it.

"It's been a long day," I said, heading upstairs. "Call me when it's done."

"Toni," Damien called when I was halfway up the steps.

I glanced back over my shoulder.

"Thank you for your help," he said with a slight bow.

I shrugged. "After what you did with the reapgrubs, I don't think you needed me."

"I wouldn't be so sure. Eric said that when he saw your meetings with Prince Kalyll in your mind, they seemed… charged with something."

"What is that supposed to mean?"

"The Fae have their own magic, Toni. They are especially talented in seeing the future. Perhaps, he knows something we don't."

"That's ridiculous."

Damien shrugged. "Could be, but I wasn't wrong in letting you do the talking, was I?"

"No, but that doesn't mean he would have said 'no' if *you* had done the talking."

He smiled, a rarity for him. "Fair enough. I should have something in two or three days."

Wow, that was fast. I breathed a sigh of relief for Aaron and Josh, but still felt impatient to bring them the good news.

I found my Camaro parked outside and felt great relief when I sank into the driver's seat and smelled its familiar scents of leather cleaner and lavender air freshener. Rosalina and Jake's scents from this morning also lingered, making me feel at home even more. It was almost 11 PM, and my stomach rumbled from hunger. Damien had offered me a granola bar from his granny bag, but at the time, the reek of the reapgrubs' blood had still been too fresh in my memory, so I'd turned it down. Now, I wished I'd wolfed it down.

Before heading toward Rosalina's place, I texted her and Jake with a couple of thumbs up. They had probably been waiting on pins and needles since we'd left. I knew I would have if I'd been left behind to wait for them to return. I would've probably eaten my nails to the quick along with several bags of potato chips. My voracious appetite had only gotten worse since my wolf was set free, and stress eating was a bigger issue than ever. As a matter of fact, I needed to stop by the store to pick up more snacks. I was starting to think that a membership to a wholesale warehouse might make sense.

A moment later, Jake replied with a thumbs up of his own and nothing more, making me wonder if I'd been wrong about him worrying.

When I got to Rosalina's, she wrapped me in a hug as soon as I stepped through the door.

"I was so worried about you and Damien." She stepped back and checked me up and down. "Is he also all right?"

"He is, just wait 'til I tell you what he did."

We talked it over as I ate a late dinner of reheated beef stew and rice Rosalina had made over the weekend.

"Oh, wow, that's quite the adventure," she said when I finished telling her everything. "He must really love his daughter."

"Yeah, I get that sense, too."

"Do you think he'll really manage to make a cure for her and Josh?"

I dipped a piece of bread into my stew. "He seems pretty certain about it."

"You don't think he's deluding himself out of sheer desperation to save his daughter, do you?"

"He doesn't seem the kind of man to delude himself about

anything."

"Yeah, I guess you're right," she added as I gathered my dirty dishes.

I cleaned the table and got the dishwasher running, and after that, we sat in front of the TV with tall glasses of wine, and watched old Charmed reruns. It seemed we were both in need of some R&R. Hopefully tomorrow we would be able to focus on our work.

CHAPTER 20

The next morning, my hopes of focusing on work were dashed when Ulfen Erickson walked through the door into the agency. His red hair was slicked back and perfectly shiny. He wore a suit and tie and polished shoes that reflected the light. His usually arrogant expression was nowhere in sight, which shocked me more than his presence.

"Good morning, Ms. Sunder and…" his blue eyes flicked in Rosalina's direction.

"López," my friend said.

"Good morning, Ms. López."

Ulfen's nose twitched, and he regarded me strangely as he undoubtedly caught my scent and probably assumed I'd been sleeping with werewolves. Very deliberately, he pushed his bewilderment away and hid it behind a detached façade.

"I thought you were happily married," I said. "Or maybe you have misplaced your wife and want me to find her." I had never liked this man, and he managed to always bring Bratty Toni out.

"Not exactly," he said, rewarding my insolence with a slight smile. "I'm here for a couple of other reasons. One is to thank you for tracking Blake." He reached inside his breast pocket and pulled out a checkbook. "I would like to pay for your services."

I shook my head. "That won't be necessary. I don't want your money." I didn't say "dirty money," but I didn't need to. My tone made it quite clear.

"As you wish." He put away his checkbook. "That makes telling you the other reason I'm here a little difficult."

"You want me to track someone else," I said, venturing a guess as to why turning down his money would do that. He was probably used to paying everybody off and getting whatever he wanted. Not here.

"You're very intuitive, Ms. Sunder."

"Unless it's a mate, I'm afraid I can't help you this time."

He opened his mouth to say something, but the door behind him opened with a chime and my next-door neighbor stepped inside.

"Everything all right, Toni?" Jake asked, sizing Ulfen up as if he were a chew toy he meant to tear to pieces with his sharp teeth.

"It's fine," I said. "Mr. Erickson was just leaving."

"I know you don't like me," Ulfen said. "I know you're Stephen's friends and that contributes to your aversion to me. He and I haven't seen eye to eye in a while, but my son may not be who you think he is."

Jake's eyebrows rose, betraying his surprise. I tried to hide my own bewilderment but didn't quite manage. Noticing, Ulfen took a step closer.

"You know something, don't you?"

I pursed my lips, refusing to say anything. I didn't trust Ulfen. For all I knew, he was working with his son, pulling some elaborate prank on the whole city.

"He was trying to frame me for his kidnapping and Blake's murder," Ulfen said. "But Blake is very alive as you helped prove. Thanks to you he's behind bars and linked to rhabo trafficking."

"He wasn't trying to frame you," I said, not to defend Stephen, I knew he was guilty, but to try to figure out why Ulfen thought his own son was behind this. "He was concerned about you."

"Rest assured, Ms. Sunder, my son was behind hiring that mage, Jenson, to stage an attack against him. He also faked his own kidnapping, all in the hopes of getting rid of me. He's a good actor, don't you think?"

"What proof do you have?"

"Ever since he returned from New Orleans, Stephen hasn't been himself. His behavior has been erratic and strange. Before I was arrested, I put a tail on him, for his protection—at least that's what I thought—but I was in for a surprise and discovered that he's running an orchestrated campaign to create unrest between werewolves and vampires. The rhabo trafficking is only one part of his deranged scheme."

Surprised to find out that Ulfen was on the same page about Stephen as we were, I didn't know what to say.

Seeing that he had my complete attention, Ulfen went on. "Something isn't right about him, and I'm afraid someone might be manipulating him."

"Now," Jake said, "that just sounds like wishful thinking. First you think he's a criminal, and then you don't."

"Maybe, but it's not unheard of. He's been wearing this… pendant." He made a gesture towards his neck. "I'd never seen it before he went to New Orleans, and he seems very protective of it."

Jake made a sound in the back of his throat and raised an eyebrow.

"Do you know what he's talking about?" I asked.

Jake nodded. "I've seen it. Stephen already had it when I met him, and yes, he's protective of it. He never takes it off. He told me it was a family heirloom."

"It isn't," Ulfen assured us.

"Are you suggesting someone is controlling him through the pendant?" Rosalina asked.

"Yes, that's exactly what I'm suggesting."

She shifted in her desk chair. "Do you have any idea who?"

"I don't, but I was hoping that you could help me find out. If I could get a hold of that pendant and bring it to you, maybe you can track the person who gave it to him."

"How would you do that if he never takes it off?" I asked.

"I don't know." Ulfen shook his head, two deep frown lines appearing across his forehead. "I can figure something out."

I considered for a moment as I thought of Stephen at the mercy of some evil mastermind. If he was being controlled, I had to help him.

"That may not be necessary," I said, speaking under my breath. Everyone turned to me.

"What do you mean?" Ulfen asked.

"I really can't explain."

Rosalina and Jake frowned at me but knew better than to ask any questions in front of Ulfen. They would surely ask once he was gone, though that didn't mean I would have definite answers for them. I was going on a hunch since I didn't exactly understand how my powers were changing.

"Do you know where I can find him?" I asked.

"He has been spending a lot of time at The Chained Wolf. That would be a good place to start." The Chained Wolf was Ulfen's nightclub, a happening place for single yuppies.

Rosalina's shoulders sank noticeably, and I turned to glance at her. She didn't say anything, but I could imagine what she was thinking. She didn't want me to get involved in this—yet another distraction from our work.

"I assume he's there at night," I said. "During club hours, correct?"

Ulfen nodded.

"Well, then at least it won't interfere with my workday. I have a business to run, Mr. Erickson, and I can't abandon it every time you have family drama."

Ulfen tapped his breast pocket. "That's precisely the reason I wish to pay for your services."

"And I've told you already, I don't want your money."

"Well, if you change your mind, just let me know. And once more, thank you." He turned to leave, then stopped, giving Jake a thorough examination. "I heard you Knights are joining the Blackridge family. Congratulations." He said the last word as if he actually meant "my condolences."

Jake said nothing, didn't even acknowledge the congratulations with a nod. Instead, he looked sickened at the reminder of his impending nuptials. My own stomach did a flip as I imagined him walking down the aisle toward that simpering blonde.

She had no business messing with my wolf.

I blinked at that thought, and the possessive feeling that came over me. It made me wonder what I would do if I saw Allison Blackridge again. Murder didn't seem too far-fetched, and at this rate, life in prison didn't either.

"Not the smartest move," Ulfen said. "Craig Blackridge is not a man anyone should trust."

"Of course you would say that," Jake answered. "You don't have an allegiance with his pack. You prefer to side with Travis

Hillworth."

A lump caught in my throat at the name. Ulfen and my werewolf father had an allegiance? I hadn't known that, and from the sounds of it, it seemed that Jake had just made a pact with a bunch that went against the Ericksons and Hillworths. My head spun with the information and what it could mean.

"Watch your back, Mr. Knight," Ulfen said. "Betrayal is the predominant card in Craig Blackridge's deck." He opened the door to leave, then turned in my direction and added, "I will be at The Chained Wolf tonight, Ms. Sunder. Stephen doesn't know that I have uncovered his secret, so please, keep it that way, if you talk to him."

As he left, both Rosalina and Jake glowered at me, a million questions etched on their worried faces.

ൈ

"What is going on?" Rosalina asked as soon as the door swung closed. "What do you mean you don't have to have the pendant?"

Jake moved closer, looking as curious as Rosalina.

I gathered my thoughts, trying to figure out a way to explain all the strange things I'd been experiencing. "I'm still figuring it out, but it seems my skills are changing. I still need to talk to Damien about it. But the thing is… I've been experiencing weird visions when I touch random objects, things that seem to be associated with the objects themselves. It's a lot like what I go through when I'm in a tracking trance. I see things, and also get distinct scents and sounds."

"What about the side effects?" Rosalina asked. "Do you have those afterward?"

"No."

"Wow. That's great."

Jake frowned. "So you're thinking that if you touch Stephen's pendant, you might be able to see something."

I nodded. "It's worth a try, at least."

"You would have to be close to him," Jake said.

"Yeah, *really* close," Rosalina put in.

I shrugged. "I don't think that will be a problem. I got close before."

"Did you ever?" Rosalina said in a singsong tone.

Jake balled his hands into fists. "I don't like this plan. Stephen is dangerous."

"That sounds to me like jealousy talking, *Jakie*," I said.

"Don't call me that."

"Why not?"

He threw his hands up in the air and paced around.

"I'll go tonight," I said.

"Why don't you focus on your agency?" He spread his arms, gesturing around. "Forget about all this other crap."

"I can't," I admitted to them and to myself. "I have to help. I can't turn a blind eye to what's going on in the city, especially if it's something I might be able to stop."

"I've always admired that in you, Toni, your desire to help others, to right injustice, but the more I dig into this, the deeper the rabbit hole goes. You don't want to get caught up in it."

"But you are," I said. "And from the sounds of it, you're getting more entangled by the day."

"I have no other choice, but you do. Please, Toni. Could you listen to me for once?"

"I just did. I heard everything you said. But I make my own decisions."

He seemed to consider what to say next, glanced at Rosalina.

"Even if you drag your friends down with you?"

Ouch! He knew how to hit where it hurt the most.

To my surprise, Rosalina put him in his place.

"Uh-uh, you leave me out of this, *Mr. Knight*. I'm a grown woman, able to make my own decisions too, as you well know. No one drags me anywhere. I go voluntarily."

Um, did that mean she was willingly letting me drag her down? *Crap!*

Jake switched his attention to me and changed tactics. "I'm sure Blake told Stephen you're a werewolf, but he's not supposed to know. You're going to let him 'find out.'" He made air quotes.

"I'm done hiding who I am," I said. "So I guess the answer is *yes*."

"That might not be such a good idea."

"Why not?"

"I don't know. Any number of reasons. For one, you don't have a pack, so he may try to drag you into his."

"He might, but I'm an alpha, Jake. He can't force me to do anything I don't want to do. Besides, there's no point in trying to hide something he already knows."

"I guess not." He sighed in frustration.

"What are you worried about?"

"You, I'm worried about you. This situation is more complex than you could ever imagine. You've no idea about the intricacies of pack life and the meaning of alliances. If you do the wrong thing, you might end up with entire packs as your enemies."

"That doesn't sound good," Rosalina said, rising from her chair and sitting on the desk.

"I'm willing to take that risk if it means stopping Stephen and whoever is controlling him, if that's really what's going on here."

"I don't know." Jake shook his head. "Something doesn't feel right about any of this."

"Damn right."

He rubbed his forehead, his frustration with me on clear display. "I'll go with you tonight."

"Won't Stephen get suspicious if you're not with Blondie instead? Isn't that going to cause *you* some trouble with your new allies?"

"Very good point," Rosalina said.

"That's for me to worry about."

"Doesn't sound like a good start to your idyllic romance, *Jakie*?"

"Shut up." He pointed a large index finger straight at me, looking pissed. "Text me your plans for tonight. I'll see you at the club." He turned on his heel and left. His intoxicating scent lingered in the air, making me want to run after him, to keep him close, but no matter how much we wanted to be together, our paths seemed to be heading in completely different directions.

CHAPTER 21

I was killing it in my tight black shorts, silky white top, and mid-thigh boots. I could feel confidence exuding off of me, and had confirmation that it was working. The eyes of Skew and Stale males alike followed my trajectory toward the bar. My steps matched the beat of the music. My pink-tipped hair swayed behind me, brushing my shoulders.

When I got to the bar, I ordered a whiskey sour and took small sips as I watched the crowd. The scene was pretty much the same as when I was here the first time with Jake. A large dance floor, a DJ as the focal point, and professional dancers performing atop platforms. On the closest platform, one of the male dancers provocatively undulated like a snake. He was covered in fur, his face partly shifted, appearing more werewolf than human. He wiggled his tongue at me when he caught me watching.

I sensed the moment Jake moved within my line of vision. Almost of their own accord, my eyes drifted over the crowd until I spotted him. His gaze immediately locked with mine, and he headed in my direction, his confident air causing many to stare in his wake. His entire demeanor screamed strength and determination, and people took notice.

He was a specimen of a man, tall and broad shouldered with a narrow waist and hips. His face was chiseled to perfection, and his eyes—those silver eyes unlike any I had ever seen—were spellbinding, like a love potion no one could resist, especially me. He wore faded jeans, a white shirt rolled up to his elbows that exposed his powerful forearms, and a black vest that hugged his torso tightly. Two buttons were undone at the top of his shirt, revealing an expanse of smooth, tanned skin I ached to touch. His scent of pine and rain mixed with the smell of clean soap made me think of our bodies pressed together under the spray of a hot shower. I had enjoyed him that way a few times, and my legs trembled at the memory.

He stopped a couple of paces from me, his eyes sweeping the length of my body, and pausing for a long moment on my breasts. Then they slowly climbed up the column of my throat to finally meet my gaze.

"You look beautiful," he said.

"You don't look too bad yourself."

He came closer and stood next to me as he ordered a drink.

"Scotch. Neat." When the drink came, he tasted it, then leaned closer to whisper in my ear. "Have you seen him?"

I shook my head and inhaled the scent of alcohol on his breath. It was stupid to spend money on drinks when we couldn't get drunk, but it still tasted good. It would taste even better on his lips.

"How about Ulfen?" I asked.

Jake inclined his head toward a raised area I hadn't noticed before. It was a sort of loft encased in glass that afforded a full view of the club. Ulfen sat there, surveying his domain. His attention drifted over us as if we weren't there, though something told me he was quite aware of every single individual in sight, especially Jake and me.

I clinked my glass against Jake's. "To your upcoming nuptials."

"Please, don't." His eyes darkened and his expression grew glum, making me realize he was truly unhappy about his situation.

"Maybe I can help you figure out how to—"

"Jake! Toni!" An enthusiastic voice said behind us.

We turned to find Stephen smiling at us, his arms extended as if to encompass both of us in one big hug.

"What are you two doing here?" he asked.

"I heard you've been spending a lot of time here lately," Jake said, "and I convinced Toni to come visit since we hadn't seen you in some time. She works too much and is in desperate need of some fun."

"I'm so glad you came." He shook Jake's hand, then gave me a quick hug, smiling all the while, looking genuinely happy to see us, his blue eyes giving nothing away.

As he pulled away from me, he held me at arm's length, his nostrils widening as he took in my new scent.

"What do I…?"

I smiled sheepishly. "It's a damn long story, but it turns out I'm a werewolf."

His jaw fell open, then mechanically closed again. "You're what?"

"Quite the shocker, huh?" Jake said.

"How is that even possible?"

"I can tell you everything over a couple of drinks and a slow dance." I winked and tucked a strand of hair behind my ear, using the full power of my female charms.

"That sounds lovely and… interesting. Of course!" He added with a charming smile that might have disengaged my panties in a previous life.

"I've already heard the whole story," Jake said in a bored tone. "I'll leave you two to it while I find that hot redhead I saw when I came in."

Stephen crossed his arms, giving Jake a sidelong glance. "Aren't you supposed to be engaged?"

Jake thumbed his nose. "Exactly. Better have some fun while I can."

He ambled away, sipping his scotch as he searched the crowd.

"There's a quiet booth in the back where we can sit," Stephen said.

"Perfect."

He smiled with brilliant perfect teeth, then crooked a finger beckoning the bartender. "Tell the chef to send some of his best appetizers."

"On it." The bartender did a military salute and disappeared through a set of doors in the back.

"The perks of being the owner's son, huh?" I teased.

"Can't complain."

We made our way to the booth and sat comfortably, watching the crowd for a bit. He focused on a dark-skinned dancer contorting herself around a pole and her beautiful, athletic body on display. She was a work of art.

"She's something else," I said.

"Isn't she? I hired her just the other day."

I swirled the liquid inside my tumbler and watched it reflect the light. "It seems you're settling nicely into your responsibilities as heir. You don't feel your father's trying to stifle you anymore?"

"I don't. He was right all along. I needed to grow up. Besides, it's not like it can't be fun." He twirled a finger to indicate our very fun surroundings.

"Lucky you."

"Yes, very lucky. Look." He held both hands up and wiggled ten fingers. "They were able to grow my finger back."

"Wow," I managed in a small breath. I couldn't help but wonder if it had ever been cut. Maybe it had all been a trick.

We were silent for a moment, then he grew serious and said, "They found Blake, did you hear?"

I almost choked and had to make a big effort to meet his eyes and answer. His expression was open and candid, looking nothing like someone who wanted to catch me in a lie. But he had to know Jake and I were responsible for Blake's capture. Blake must have told him.

"Um, I saw something in the news. It's crazy. How is he alive? I saw his body…" I trailed off, hoping I wasn't overdoing it.

He knew I was aware Blake wasn't dead, but he didn't know that *I* knew he knew that Jake and I had been the ones to fight Blake at the warehouse. *Witchlights!* That gave me a headache.

He scratched his beard. "I can't understand it either. The police are investigating. Hopefully, they'll find out why he did all of this. I trusted him, Toni. My father trusted him, and Blake betrayed all of us."

So that was the story he was trying to sell me, Blake did everything on his own, and Stephen was an innocent little lamb.

"What a bastard," I said. "People like that… someone should put a bullet in their brains."

I examined his face for the slightest hint that might betray his act. He knew *I* had been the one to almost kill his henchmen and ruin his little rhabo trip, but he gave nothing away, not the slightest twitch of his mouth or resentful hint in his gaze. Was he really that good of an actor? Or could Ulfen be right? Could someone be controlling him? Maybe he wasn't aware of what he was doing.

Vampires could use their compulsion powers on Stales, but not on shifters of any kind, so a mage would have to be behind any sort of manipulation.

"But enough of that." Stephen waved a hand around. "Tell me about you. How is any of this possible?" He twitched his nose to indicate my wolf scent.

"Blame my mother for it."

A huge platter of appetizers got delivered to our booth: bruschettas, fried calamari, stuffed mushrooms, and tomato and mozzarella skewers.

We ate a bit before I proceeded to tell him about my discovery, though with as little detail as possible. In the end, he looked shocked, his mouth slightly parted, and his words nowhere to be found for a few beats. Once more, the acting was on point.

At last, he spoke. "I'm sorry to say this, Toni, but your mother did you a great injustice."

"I know. The more I learn, the more I realize that."

I felt as if I was just starting to scratch the surface of my werewolf potential. On top of that, there were the changes happening to my tracking skills. There was no telling how much different my life would be if my mom had been honest from the beginning. Maybe Jake and I would be together and not fated to forever be apart from each other, with him marrying someone he didn't love.

A shroud of gloom seemed to fall over me as my thoughts followed the dark path of what could have been. Stephen's face drew into a sympathetic expression, dashed with a hint of pity. That snapped me back into the moment, and I shook my head, reminded of the reason I was here.

"But enough of me." I waved a hand in the air the way he had. "How about that dance you promised me?"

"Are you sure you don't want to talk about it some more?" he asked as if he were some sort of therapist and not a drug lord, willing or not.

"I'm sure." I danced on the spot, wiggling my torso and arms. "I'm here for some fun."

His concerned expression changed to something slightly predatory, and he answered in a voice an octave deeper. "Fun with you is the best kind."

We moved onto the dance floor. People made way for us as they noticed Stephen. They ogled him as if he were some sort of celebrity, and I registered the jealous glances that both men and women sent in my direction.

The song the DJ was playing was some dubstep with a strong baseline that rattled in my chest. I began moving to the rhythm of the beat, swaying my hips and weaving my arms as if I were a spell-wielding mage. Out of the corner of my eye, I noticed Jake dancing with the redhead he'd mentioned. She was practically hanging off of him, rubbing her entire front against his body as if she were a human windshield wiper.

My rage, which I had managed to keep in check during the last few days, reared its ugly head. A tingling sensation rippled from my shoulders all the way down to my hands and sharp claws sprang at the tips of my fingers.

I balled my hands into fists to hide my reaction from Stephen. He inclined his head, leaning closer. "It seems impossible," he said in a rumbling voice, "but you're even hotter than before."

He wrapped an arm around my waist and pulled me against him. I placed my fists on his chest and slowly allowed my fingers to spread open. The claws were gone, and I did my best not to glance in Jake's direction.

"And I can feel you're as strong as ever." I let my fingers

explore his firm pecs, teasing his nipples on my way up toward his neck.

He shivered and smiled, his eyes growing hooded, while, under his shirt, I felt a thick chain. Pressing his nose to my hair, he inhaled deeply and ground his hips into mine. I felt his hardness through the thin fabric of my shorts and fought the urge to push him away. Instead, I wrapped one hand around the nape of his neck while I allowed the other to follow the trail of the chain. Finally, my fingers found the pendant Jake and Ulfen had mentioned.

As I tried to feel the trinket through his shirt, I noticed Jake march off the dance floor. The redhead was hot on his heels, appearing confused. He looked pissed. I smiled. Apparently, I wasn't the only one experiencing a bit of jealous rage, except he'd opted to leave rather than bare it.

Serves him right.

Shaking all thoughts of Jake aside, I tried to concentrate on touching the pendant through Stephen's shirt, but I got no vibes of any kind from it. I needed to be able to touch it directly. Hoping he wouldn't notice, I worked to undo one of the buttons of his shirt—except, he didn't miss a beat and made a sound in the back of his throat as he noticed my daring move. Of course, he took it the wrong way and concluded I had the hots for him.

So not *the case.*

In fact, bile was starting to rise up my throat. He had helped Blake hurt Jake at the warehouse. They had almost killed him. If I hadn't been there, I had a feeling Jake would be dead now, and we would have found no trace of his body to even bury or use for evidence to find the culprit.

My rage rekindled like a stubborn forest fire that wouldn't be put out.

I didn't yet know if I should hate Stephen or not, but, as he pressed his body against mine, all I wanted to do was punch him in the jaw.

Reigning in my anger, I snuck my fingers through the gap I'd created in his shirt. They touched something cold and intricate. I closed my eyes trying to focus, but Stephen snatched my hand and pressed it to his lips.

"I'm so glad you came," he said. "I've been wanting to see you, but I've been so busy. Ever since I came back from New Orleans, my life has been a whirlwind."

I smiled up at him, syrupy sweet. "How come?"

"With my father in jail, I've had to focus on the family business. Now that he's out, though, I hope I'll have more time to see you, if you would like to, which I'm getting the feeling you would."

My saccharine smile deepened. "I've been busy too, but I look forward to it. We should both try to make time to—"

Without warning, Stephen lowered his lips to mine and kissed me. His tongue slipped into my mouth, tasting of alcohol and basil. I resisted the urge to gag, kissed him back for a millisecond, then pulled away. He growled in the back of his throat and got ready to kiss me again, but the clear sound of glass breaking rose over the music's bass.

Stephen glanced up, and I followed his gaze. We couldn't quite see what had happened through the mass of dancing bodies, but it seemed one of the staff had dropped a tray of glasses, and they had smashed on the floor. Jake stood nearby, towering over everyone, his clear gaze smoldering with anger. Something told me he had seen that kiss and had caused a ruckus to create a distraction.

Taking advantage of the moment, I slipped my fingers under Stephen's shirt once more, and touched the pendant.

A slew of images tumbled into my mind, crashing into one

another, overwhelming me with the speed at which they appeared. Their colors were strident and discordant like a symphony of rainbows on steroids. Behind all the clashing colors, I perceived the outline of shapes. Objects, faces, buildings, but the images blurred, indistinguishable and useless.

Even after the onslaught should've stopped, it continued with a hammering quality that threatened to split my skull in two. I yanked my hand away from the pendant and pressed it to my forehead, staggering backward, suddenly weak-limbed and dizzy. Stephen caught me just in time before I fell.

"Toni!" He swept me off my feet and carried me off of the dance floor.

I blinked drunkenly as the sea of bodies parted to let us through, some of them gaping while others seemed to swoon at my knight in shining armor's chivalry. He brought me back to the booth, sat me down, and squatted in front of me. Holding one of my hands in his, he stared up with concern.

"Are you all right?"

"I'm fine," I lied, taking a deep breath as I tried to convince myself that the club was not spinning on its axis.

"You can't be drunk," he said, sounding a bit suspicious.

"Oh, no. It's not that. I'm… it's just I'm still experiencing some… side effects from the spell."

"Damn, that sucks."

"It does."

I laid a hand over my eyes and breathed deeply, willing the after images of my vision to go away. The colors blended into each other as if some psychedelic artist was using my mind as a canvas and was bent on blinding me with every known hue in the universe.

"Toni, what happened?" Jake had arrived, but I couldn't look at him, so I kept my hand over my eyes.

"She says it's the side effects from the spell," Stephen offered. "She just started to fall. I caught her just in time."

Jake had the sense not to ask what side effects and played along. "How bad is it this time, Toni?"

I held my free hand up in a "wait a minute" gesture and said nothing. I was afraid that if I spoke I would throw up, and it would be as nasty as all the merging colors inside my head. Rainbow puke at its best.

Slowly, the colors fell away, and when they were all gone, a single image remained.

It was a symbol etched in rough black lines, depicting a triangular shape with what looked like a knife or dagger inside of it. The weapon pierced the bottom of the triangle and was tipped by what might be an upside down cross.

I blinked my eyes open and stared straight into Jake's silver gaze. His face was pinched in concern, his full lips pursed in concentration as if he were willing me to be better at once. I gave him a nod and a quick smile, then turned my attention to Stephen who was still squatting in front of me, his hand resting on my knee.

I squeezed his fingers. "I'm better now. Thank you. I'm sorry for…" I waved my hand about.

"There's nothing to be sorry about. I just hope you're okay."

"I am. It's the—"

A loud bang and screams suddenly erupted at the front of the club. Stephen jumped to his feet and whirled around. Jake was already facing the other direction, standing at a slight crouch. The DJ and the performers froze as clubgoers suddenly stampeded toward the back of the building, trampling each other.

I rose from the booth, my eyes darting all around, searching for the cause of the panic. My gaze zeroed in on a pale figure grabbing a woman by the neck and tearing into her throat. Behind him, others rushed in, indiscriminately attacking patrons.

An army of vampires on a killing spree had invaded The Chained Wolf.

CHAPTER 22

Loud music continued to boom through the giant speakers as chaos unfolded. Strobe lights and dancing spotlights went on their merry way highlighting the massacre.

The vampires blurred in and out of existence, attacking one person after another, while the revelers tried to climb over each other toward the back emergency exit, screaming and stumbling like drunken toddlers.

The bouncers who had stood inconspicuously in different corners of the club peeled away from their watching places and shifted from human-shaped protectors into massive werewolves.

From his spot in the observation room, Ulfen also jumped into action, leaping down the steps and shifting in mid-air. His wolf was large and tawny, the fur matching his human hair in shade. Round, blue eyes flashed in my direction as he leaped over several tables heading toward the swarm of vampires in the front.

Without a word, Jake shifted and charged, too, disappearing in the fray. When he reached the dance floor, he took a final leap and disappeared into the turmoil, his tail waving like a war flag in his wake.

Stephen turned toward me and grabbed me by the wrist. "I have to get you out of here," he said, attempting to pull me toward the exit where people were pushing, shoving, and stepping on whoever stood in their way to get there first.

I yanked my arm free. "We have to help."

"No, Toni, you don't stand a chance against a vampire. I have to take you to safety." He tried to grab me again, but I pulled back and shifted in one swift motion, my hands turning to paws as I dropped to the floor, my outfit splitting down my back, and disappearing under a table as I tossed it aside with a snap of my teeth and a jerk of my head.

I darted a cold glance in Stephen's direction, almost pushing a thought into his head with my alpha abilities.

Fight, you coward, I wanted to say, but he couldn't know I was an alpha. If he learned that bit of information, he would realize that I knew his game, that I'd heard Blake call for his help at the warehouse. So instead, I followed in Jake's steps, leaping over several tables and diving into the chaos.

When I landed in the middle of the dance floor, my eyes roved all around, searching for a target. I found one quickly, a vamp wearing a black tank top, his corded arms naked and bulging with dark veins. He had one of the performers in his grip, a man dressed in nothing but glittering shorts and silver paint that highlighted his muscles.

The vamp bent over the dancer and clamped his jaw around the man's throat. His eyes rolled to the back of his head as he drank his victim's blood, lost in ecstasy.

Fearing it might be too late for the dancer, I lunged forward, ready to tear the monster in two. I closed my jaw around the vamp's thigh, gnashing my teeth together. He roared and let go of his victim, who dropped to the floor clutching his neck. I darted a glance in his direction, glad to see he was still alive.

As the vamp turned his attention to me, I jerked my head downward and almost managed to yank him to the floor, but he was strong and remained on his feet. Baring his fangs with a hiss, he went for my neck with blood-stained claws.

I retreated with a backward jump, growling and locking eyes with the beast. We circled each other for a moment, then he came at me. I leaped out of the way and, as he flew by, I chomped on his forearm with all my strength. Sinew and bone crunched like wood as his arm broke off from the elbow down, leaving behind a splintered stump. I expected blood to spurt out like water from a hose but barely a few drops dripped to the floor despite the dark veins that still bulged at his biceps.

He fell to his knees, screaming like a madman, staring at the stump, then back at the rest of his arm still caught between my teeth.

Spitting in disgust, I let the limb drop. A sour stench rose from the dismembered arm, and I recognized its awful tang immediately. It was the smell of rhabo-infected vamp flesh—if what I'd bitten off could be called that.

Hissing in anger, the vampire crawled toward his severed arm. With trembling fingers, he snatched it up, turned it this way and that, then stuck it to his splintered stump. I stared in horror as the bulging veins writhed with the creature's dark blood, finding the connection to their severed counterparts and rejoining. Right before my eyes, the limb reattached itself with a wet sound, then the vampire wiggled his fingers and smiled with satisfaction.

A chair went flying above my head and crashed against the wall behind me. Quickly, I glanced around the room, looking for Jake. Half of the patrons seemed to have found their way out of the club, while the other half still fought to reach the emergency exit. Finally, I spotted Jake fighting against a vampire with tattoos all over his bald head. Jake's silver eyes met mine for an instant as he leaped against a concrete column, flew toward his opponent, and slashed his sharp claws across the vamp's neck.

I returned my attention to my still-kneeling opponent, who was grinning like mad. Blood stained his sharp fangs. Making a big show, he raked his claws down his chest, ripping off his black tank top and discarding it on the floor. He flexed both arms in unison, shook his head with a satisfied growl, then glared at me, hatred and murder burning in his eyes.

Crap! I pissed him off.

He seemed to float to a standing position. I shook my head and gave him a wolfish grin, letting him know I was ready for more. He bared his throat in a bloodcurdling roar. I rolled my eyes. Cool how I could still do it in my wolf form.

Was the vamp's plan to kill me with high decibels? Hadn't he realized we were at a nightclub with speakers as big as refrigerators standing at either end? Clearly, his bark was worse than his bite.

I was about to jump him and take care of his loud mouth when two other vamps peeled away from the fight and joined my attacker.

Oh, shit!

Okay, so the roar had been to call his pals to help him? I had to remember that one.

With his friends by his side, Loud Mouth grew a pair and started advancing in my direction. I took several steps back until I hit the wall and stopped next to a broken chair. The three vampires formed a semicircle, trapping me. I snapped my teeth left, right, and center, warning them to stay away.

The one on the left lunged at me and as I jumped to the right, the other one was waiting for me. At once, they sank their claws into my back, bearing their entire weight down on me. I yelped as pain flared along my spine, and my legs gave out under the pressure.

I struggled to get free, snapping my teeth and bucking, but my efforts were in vain. Loud Mouth stalked closer, smiling like the cat that ate an entire dairy aisle full of cream. I whimpered, a cry of help to anyone who would hear. But the sound was completely useless in the wake of the thumping bass still raging over the cries of battle.

Yet, Jake appeared behind Loud Mouth, ready to attack—except a fourth vampire flew out of nowhere and crashed into him. They rolled away in a snarling pile, knocking down chairs and tables like bowling pins.

Loud Mouth cracked his neck and prepared to jump me. An image flashed before my eyes: my body limp on the floor, my wolf head in one of Loud Mouth's hands as he licked the fingers of the other, one at a time.

I was about to die, and it wouldn't be pretty.

My vision snapped back into focus and—as the vamp blurred before my eyes, his hands outstretched, ready to twist my head off its perch—I instinctively went for one of my favorite tricks.

I shifted into my human form.

CHAPTER 23

It was madness to abandon my wolf in favor of my human form. I couldn't tell what prompted me to do it, but it felt right.

My body unfurled, elongating, changing shapes. The hands that held me down lost their grip, fingers slipping on blood-slippery skin. Loud Mouth was taken aback for an instant, but as he got over his surprise and adjusted his attack to my new shape, I thrust my hands forward, meeting his palms with mine, interlacing my fingers with his, and squeezing with all my strength.

He scrunched up his face, confused, an expression of "what the hell?" shaping his features. I was asking myself the same question when, purely on reflex, I conjured back all the overwhelming colors, sounds, and sensations of my earlier vision and pushed them forward, using my alpha communication ability as if it were a ramrod.

Energy coursed through my body, surging from my mind, traveling up my arms, and flowing into Loud Mouth like high-voltage electricity. He screamed, throwing his head back, and thrashing as if he was having a seizure. The two vamps that held me jumped back, crying out, and shaking their hands as if they'd been burned.

Red, shimmering energy flowed down my hands and passed into the vampire until he went limp and moved no more.

I let go of his hands and, still glowing, rose to my feet. As if possessed, I glanced back and forth between the remaining attackers. One of them stared at the fallen vamp, then back at me, his eyes brimming with fear and infinite questions. I made as if to grab him, and he turned tail, ran toward one of the front windows, and crashed through it. Shards of glass sprayed all around as he disappeared down the sidewalk. I turned to my remaining attacker, and it only took one look from me to send him running the way of his leech friend.

Feeling the way I did in a trance, I glanced all around me. The music sounded distant. The strobing lights twirled and danced all around, drawing my eyes this way and that. Broken bodies and smashed furniture littered the floor. Puddles of dark blood reflected the light, looking like bottomless wells.

I caught sight of my toes. They were shining from within. I lifted my hands. They glowed, too.

Wow, I'm a light bulb, I mused.

My skin tingled as the energy slowly sputtered out, then disappeared.

At the sound of police sirens, the remaining vampires escaped in a blur of movement. Several wolves took chase, and the sounds of battle quickly died out, leaving behind only the thumping of the music.

I knew I should hunker down behind a table to hide my naked body, but all I could do was stare at a fixed point on the floor, my mind a kaleidoscope of pretty colors.

The music suddenly died with a whine of feedback. Jake ran to my side in his wolf form, his eyes dark with the aftermath of the battle. He checked me up and down, looking for injuries.

"I'm all right," I said in a mechanical voice.

He pressed his big head to my stomach, exhaling a sigh of relief. I laid my hands on his soft fur, and found comfort in petting him.

Ulfen marched in our direction, wearing a burgundy, silken robe. I blinked, the absurd sight waking me from my stupor. He looked like freaking Hugh Hefner. He held another similar robe in his hands with a pair of slippers on top. He handed them over.

"Here," he said, keeping his blue eyes focused on mine, for which I was grateful. Maybe he knew that if his gaze had headed south, I would've tried to claw his eyes out.

I threw the slippers on the floor and put them on as I stuffed my arms into the silken robe and tied it around my waist. Over Ulfen's shoulder, I saw others running around in Hugh Hefner robes, busying themselves with righting furniture and pushing bodies out of the way. It seemed they were prepared for naked eventualities, a smart thing for werewolves to do. I took note.

"Want a robe, Knight?" Ulfen asked.

Jake shook his head and bared his teeth. He seemed to be in a protective mood and preferred his wolf shape for the job.

Ulfen shrugged. "Have it your way, but let's get out of here before the police arrive. This way." He trudged toward the back of the building, swerving through bodies and debris. I grabbed my clutch from the booth where I'd left it. My ID and Camaro keys were in it. Man, I would have to figure out a way to keep those on me when I shifted.

I glanced down at Jake, questioningly. He gave one nod, so I followed. Jake walked protectively at my side, his claws clicking on the floor. Ulfen led us through the kitchen where the smell of fried food clogged the air. No one was there. Potatoes cut into wedges were turning brown on the prep station, and a pot bubbled madly on an industrial-sized stove. Ulfen ignored all of it and exited through a metal door into the back alley. It was a different exit from the one Jake and I had used to sneak in last time, but it led to the same narrow alleyway.

A black sedan already waited there, the engine running. Ulfen opened the back door for me. I climbed in, Jake right behind me. The door slammed shut, and Ulfen climbed in the passenger seat.

"Downtown," he told the driver.

The man nodded and we were off.

Jake lay across the seat and rested his head on my lap. His massive body occupied most of the space while I was pushed against the door. I didn't mind, though. It felt warm and cozy and safe.

No one said anything during the fifteen-minute drive. When we arrived at a tall building close to Busch Stadium, we went into an underground parking lot, and the driver deposited us right in front of an elevator. We climbed in, and Ulfen pressed the top number on the row of buttons and waved a security card in front of a reader.

The elevator went straight up without stops, and it opened into a lavish foyer. He led us to a luxurious living room furnished with white leather couches overlooking floor-to-ceiling windows with a breathtaking view of the city.

"Sit, Ms. Sunder." He pointed toward one of the sofas, then disappeared into an adjacent room.

I did as I was told, still feeling addled and not quite myself, like I'd just woken up from a long nap and needed a double espresso.

"This place is something, huh?" I said.

Jake hopped on the sofa and, again, laid his head on my lap.

A well-stocked bar was tucked in a corner of the room. I sighed. "I wouldn't mind a stiff drink that would actually dull the edge for more than two seconds. I mean… the stuff tastes good, but it's pretty much useless," I said, staring longingly at the bottles lining the glass shelves against the wall.

Ulfen returned, dressed in slacks and a button up shirt. A pile of clothes rested in his hands. He set them on the sofa across from where we sat and walked back toward the bar.

"I've got just the thing for you, Ms. Sunder." He poured a red liquid in three tumblers, walked back to the sofa, and set them on the glass coffee table between us. He pushed two of the tumblers in our direction, then sat and sipped from his, tiredly rubbing his neck.

I picked up the red drink and took a sip. It smelled of oak and earthy moss, and burned all the way down. I coughed and thumped my chest. Warmth spread through my body, and I felt my shoulders relax a bit.

"That's some good stuff," I said. "What is it?"

"It's called Oakfire. It's not cheap." He swirled the liquid, glancing at it against the light.

"Figures. I also want one of those shifting rings, but they're not cheap either."

Ulfen raised an eyebrow. "Shifting rings are not only expensive but rare." He wiggled his fingers to show he didn't have one.

"Oh." Eric hadn't mentioned that.

He set his glass down. "Well, did you find anything out?"

"That your son is a coward," I said. "He left as soon as the battle began."

"I noticed."

I sighed and set the tumbler down next to Jake's. "Let me change first, then I'll try to explain what I saw when I touched his pendant." I gestured toward the pile of clothes.

Ulfen handed them over, and as I stood, he pointed toward the corridor to my back. "There's a powder room that way."

I found the room and locked the door behind me. The space was ample and well-stocked with embroidered hand towels and tiny soaps in a porcelain dish right by a large vessel sink.

I picked a pair of sweats and a baggy T-shirt and felt glad to be rid of the silky robe. It had felt icky against my skin for some reason. One hundred percent cotton was more my thing.

The memory of my glowing body flashed before my eyes. Neither Jake nor Ulfen had brought it up, so maybe I'd been the only one able to see my Christmas tree impersonation. I really hoped so because I would have no idea what to tell them if they started asking questions. I needed to talk to Damien before I drew any conclusions. He was the only one who could help explain my situation. I pushed the memories away, stamping them down flat at the bottom of my list of things to worry about. They probably needed to be at the very top, but I just couldn't deal with them right now.

"Jake," I said when I returned to the living room, "I left the rest of the clothes by the sink. Go change. I think we're safe here."

Reluctantly, he hopped off the couch and went into the bathroom. He was back in a matter of seconds, also wearing sweats and a T-shirt, except in his case, they didn't drape over his body like curtains, but hugged his firm muscles tightly, especially his fine butt.

He sat next to me again and, for a moment, I wished he would put his head back on my lap so I could run my fingers through his silky light brown hair, but that wasn't going to happen. In fact, he sat at the other end of the sofa, making me feel bereft.

"So… did it work?" Ulfen asked. "Were you able to figure out who gave him the pendant?"

I shook my head. "I wasn't. I'm sorry."

Jake turned his body to face me. "But you said you saw something?"

"I did. There was actually a lot, but it was all behind a veil of color, so I couldn't tell what any of it was. It was overwhelming. It made me weak and gave me a horrible headache. Stephen had to carry me back to the booth."

Both Jake and Ulfen nodded. They had witnessed my little fainting spell, which made me feel like such a wimp.

"But then, at the end," I continued, "there was a moment when all the colors cleared and I saw a weird shape. It's nothing I've ever seen before, but it was like…" I tried to think of how to explain it, then realized it would be a lot easier if I drew it. "Do you have pen and paper?" I asked Ulfen.

He gave a nod and stood. A moment later, he was back from the bar with a yellow legal pad and an ink pen.

I drew the symbol I'd seen in my mind's eye the best I could: a triangle with a dagger inside of it. I was no artist, but I wasn't even done sketching it out when Ulfen inhaled sharply. My pen stopped. Jake and I both glanced up.

"What is it?" Jake asked. "Do you recognize it?"

Ulfen nodded and swallowed thickly. The color drained from his face, and he stood up and started pacing in front of the sofa.

After a few beats of silence, Jake grew irritated. "So are you going to tell us about it? Or what?"

Ulfen stopped by the windows and peered out into the night, hands poised on his waist. "We need to call for a meeting of the Pack Rule."

"What?!" Jake exclaimed incredulously, rising to his feet. His wide-eyed expression made my heart pick up its beat. He didn't spook easily.

I swallowed thickly. "What's the Pack Rule?"

"It's a group of wolf leaders formed by the alphas of all the packs in a certain territory," Jake answered. "Every city has its own group, and they all answer to the Supreme Pack Rule, which has been around for a very long time. Pack Rules come together when the safety of their territories is threatened." He directed his attention toward Ulfen. "Our Pack Rule hasn't convened in several years. Why would some symbol require them to meet?"

I imagined a bunch of geriatric alpha's arguing with each other. Not a pleasant thought.

Ulfen slowly turned away from the windows. When he faced us, his expression was pinched and unhappy. "That's not just *some* symbol, Knight. As harmless as it may seem, it's heresy, and it represents the worst possible crime among supernaturals."

I glanced between the two alphas, my heart racing as I sensed the tension building between them. For Skews to call anything heresy, it had to be bad.

"That symbol," Ulfen said, "is used to represent hybrid packs."

CHAPTER 24

"The what?!" I exclaimed. I didn't know what "hybrid pack" meant, but it sure sounded like heresy.

Among Stales hybrid things were normally good like Prius cars or cotton candy grapes. Those things were wholesome, but a hybrid pack sounded like nothing but trouble.

Jake let out a sharp exhale, then met my gaze. The expression of horror etched on his face sent a chill down my spine.

"Ulfen is talking about a werewolf who is also a vampire," he said with a shudder that he disguised as a roll of his shoulders.

"Um, I thought that was impossible," I said, subconsciously lifting a hand to my neck. "I thought werewolves were immune to vampire venom."

"And we are." Ulfen walked away from the windows and took a seat across from me again. "Unless," he pointed toward the sketch I'd made, which still lay unfinished on the coffee table, "unless the Unholy Vessel has been unearthed."

He let that sink in, and sink it did. I felt as if I'd swallowed a ten-pound pill.

"You see," he continued, "legend has it that hundreds of years ago, a powerful mage created a vessel and infused it with a spell of his own creation. He lived in a town ravaged by both werewolves and vampires. One day, after a long journey, he came back to find his entire family slaughtered by vampires. His wife, five children, and elderly mother had been drained then torn to pieces. After grieving for weeks, he vowed revenge against the coven that killed his family. He became obsessed, crazy, his neighbors said. He rarely came out of his house. Years went by, and he became an old man. Everyone had discounted him, forgotten about him. But he never stopped working on his revenge.

"It took him over thirty years to perfect the spell he put on the vessel, but he did it. The accounts of how he created the first hybrid vary. Some say he captured a weak vampire, drained him of his blood, then tricked a pack of werewolves to drink the blood. Others claimed that he found willing participants, that he told them drinking vampire blood from the vessel would make them stronger.

"Whatever the case, after every member of the pack drank from the tainted blood, they did grow stronger, but also became the mage's slaves. They were monstrous—not wolves anymore but revolting creatures given to carnage.

"The spell allowed the mage to control them. But that wasn't all, they also became hungry for blood, insatiable, willing to go to any lengths to get it. The mage used this hunger and wildness to his advantage. He sent the pack to destroy the coven that had killed his family. The hybrids were so strong they didn't have any trouble with their task. They killed every single vampire, including the eldest and strongest among them. But when they were done with the coven, their hunger was far from satiated, so they went back to the town and massacred every single resident, including the mage who, in his madness, relished the chaos he'd caused and welcomed his death with open arms.

"After that, the hybrids went their separate ways, killing whoever they encountered. It took a concerted effort from several packs to hunt them all down and kill them. Afterward, they tried to destroy the Unholy Vessel, but it was impossible. So they hid it, buried it somewhere. This symbol," he pulled the paper closer and examined it with weary eyes, "was created as a warning. It represents the mage's creation and reminds werewolves of what can happen if the vessel fell in the wrong hands."

Ulfen's voice rang in the air even after he stopped talking. I rubbed my arms, trying to dispel the chills that were sprouting goose bumps over my skin.

Jake ran stiff fingers into his hair, looking as unsettled as I felt. "I think now I remember my grandfather telling me something about it when I was little."

"For generations the warning has been getting weaker and weaker," Ulfen said. "My ancestors, however, were involved in the hunting of those hybrids, so the message has been passed down with more persistence than in other families."

"Do you know where the item is supposed to be hidden?" I asked as I tried to get my insides to go from Jell-O back to something more solid.

Ulfen shook his head. "No, that knowledge died with the man who buried the vessel. Or at least, it was supposed to."

"This… doesn't necessarily mean that someone has found the vessel," I said. "Maybe, for some reason, Stephen was just thinking about it when I touched the necklace."

"It seems unlikely," Jake said. "I personally think he was preoccupied with grabbing your ass."

Ulfen made a face and cut a glance between Jake and me.

"Don't look at me like that," Jake said. "Stephen still likes her, whether or not you think he should do better than a tracker."

Clearing his throat, Ulfen twisted in his seat. "I admit I told my son something to that effect, but that was well over a year ago. My opinion of Ms. Sunder has drastically changed."

"Has it?" I cocked my head to one side and gave him a questioning stare.

"Yes, it has." He stood, rounded the sofa, and placed his hands on the head rest. "Even more now that I know you're a fierce werewolf."

I rolled my eyes. Of course, that was all that mattered to him. Next, he would ask me who my father was and then his opinion of me would really soar.

"I bet it has," Jake put in.

"That's neither here nor there." Ulfen reached for a telephone that rested on the bar top. "We need to call the Pack Rule members and tell them about this."

"You don't think you're blowing things out of proportion just a little?" I asked. "I mean, why bother all those… nice elders and alphas?"

"On something like this, Ms. Sunder," Ulfen said as he dialed the phone number, "I'd rather be safe than sorry."

CHAPTER 25

Ulfen's driver took Jake and me back to my place. Jake insisted on accompanying me to make sure I got home safely. When I tried to dismiss him at the door, he pushed his way in, closed the door behind him, engaged the deadlock, and slid the chain into place.

"I doubt that will stop any hybrids from breaking in," I said.

"What was the glowing all about, Toni?" He gave me an unwavering, deadpan stare.

"Damn!" I whirled, stomped toward the kitchen and fed Cupid. His blue fins waved beautifully in the water as he swam to the top. "I was hoping no one had noticed that." I tapped Cupid's fishbowl, then walked to the living room, and sank onto my brand-new couch.

"Maybe Ulfen didn't, but I didn't miss a thing." He sat next to me, his shoulders angled in my direction. "Was that another… new development?"

I nodded, feeling my body wither with exhaustion—all the way from the top of my head to the tips of my toes. When would I reach a state resembling normalcy? Something seemed to change every day, throwing me for another loop before I recovered from the last one.

"You blasted that vampire with your touch," Jake said. "He didn't get back up—at least not while we were there."

"Do you think I killed him?" It was stupid to fret about that. Loud Mouth had been about to tear my head off, but I'd already killed someone, and I didn't want to add another one to my tally. Hell, I didn't want to have a tally.

"I hope you did," Jake, the insensitive ass, said.

I buried my face in my hands. There was no point trying to talk to Jake about this. He would never understand. He had been indoctrinated since childhood to believe that vampires were his mortal enemies, while I had grown up befriending every Skew I ever met. I always fit in better with them, and, growing up, some of my best friends were vampires.

He laid a hand on my back and rubbed up and down. "It's okay. I don't think you killed him. He looked dead, but don't they always? You acted in self-defense and used a new skill probably on instinct. No one could blame you if he's dead. Once you figure out all your new abilities, you'll be able to gauge better how to use them. I bet you will."

I peeled my hands away from my face and blinked up in surprise. "Who are you? And what have you done with Jacob Knight?" I demanded.

"When I couldn't get to you, I thought…" he didn't finish and was silent for a moment. Then he said something random, "You were there."

I frowned.

"At the repair shop when we *rescued* Stephen." He smiled sadly.

"Oh, yeah, you figured that out."

He nodded. "Your wolf is beautiful. I realized it when I saw you fight."

Tenderly, he started caressing my jaw with his thumb. My eyelids fluttered at his touch. I closed my eyes and enjoyed the caress, knowing full well that I shouldn't, that I should pull away and put some distance between us. He was not only engaged. He had a pact to uphold, a promise that, if broken, could lead to his death.

That thought sobered me up, and I leaned away from his touch. "You should leave. It's not a good idea for you to be here."

"I know, but I don't want to leave. I want to stay here with you to talk and kiss and make love." His eyes trembled with emotion.

A lump got caught in my throat. "You shouldn't say those things."

"Only because they are true." He pressed his forehead to mine as he resumed caressing my face, his thumb running over my eyebrow, cheekbone, and finally my lips. "I don't know how, but I'll find a way to be with you, Toni. I promise you."

I shook my head, rubbing my forehead against his. "It was a promise that got you in this mess to begin with, so don't."

"It was the *wrong* promise," he said. "I realize now that it was unfair of my father to ask me to continue the family legacy when he knew I'm more suited to be a lone wolf, at least until I met you. And it was even worse for my grandfather to maneuver me into this situation. I don't want to be a pack leader. I don't care for Allison Blackridge. I don't even like her, but Walter doesn't give a shit about that. He only cares about restoring the pack's previous grandeur, even if he steamrolls my happiness in the process. There's nothing more important to him than the Knight legacy."

"Jake." His name left my lips in a hot whisper as I pressed my hand on top of his and leaned into his touch, my eyes closing of their own accord. His warmth seeped into me like morning sunshine.

My heart was melting. Jake had never talked to me this way, with such honesty and openness. And as I measured the weight of his words, I realized I owed him the same.

"I'm a mess. My emotions, my body. My abilities are out of control, and I have no idea where any of it will lead. When this is all said and done, I may not be good for you. I may become the biggest mistake you've ever made."

"No. That's impossible. I already know what my biggest mistake was. I should have never left you, Toni. I should've stuck by you and kept you all to myself."

My heart did a flip worthy of a ten-point score.

Overwhelmed with emotion, I took his face in my hands and leaned in for a kiss. To my surprise, he pulled back, his gaze filling with regret.

"I can't," he said. "I know that if I kiss you now, I won't be able to stop. I will take you and make you mine in every way I know." His voice was husky and full of meaning.

I pressed my thighs together as a thrill ran straight through my core, making me want him more than ever.

"It wouldn't be right," he continued. "Not with this engagement and pact hanging over my head. As much as I hate it, I gave my word to Allison." He pulled away from me, looking embarrassed.

Maybe knowing that insipid blonde had a promise from Jake should have broken my heart, but instead, it made me proud of him, made me see his integrity and strength of character. He wasn't some weak man who compromised his honor for anything. And when he became mine it would be with a clean slate, with nothing to hold him back. I couldn't be angry with him for that. In fact, I admired him.

I scooted closer and teasingly nudged his shoulder with mine. "I totally get it, and guess what?" He glanced at me sideways. "I'll wait. However long it takes, I'll wait for you."

He faced me, took off his leather bracelet, and proceeded to put it around my wrist. "I want you to have it."

I ran my finger over the metal arrow motif. "It's pretty."

"The arrow… it represents you."

I glanced up, surprised. "Me?"

He nodded.

"And the new arrow tattoo around your biceps?"

"Also you. You pierced my heart through and through like the Cupid that you are."

My heart melted, forming a puddle at the bottom of my chest. How could I resist this man? We exchanged a smile. Tenderly, he leaned close and kissed the top of my head. Suddenly, he scooped me up in his arms and carried me to the bedroom.

"Wait, what are you doing?"

He laid me on the bed. "After today, you need rest. You look tired."

"Way to get my hopes up," I teased.

With one swift motion, he removed his shirt, muscles rippling. The sweatpants Ulfen had provided rode low and clung tightly to him, revealing his sizable anatomy and leaving little to the imagination. His chest was smooth and tanned. The swell of his pecs tapered down into a perfect six-pack and a V that dove south and made my mouth go dry.

"O-kay," I said, tearing my eyes away from his fine body. "So what is this? The Torture Toni Thirst Trap?"

"No, it's bedtime. Scoot over."

"Did you forget about that pact thing you were talking about just a moment ago?"

"As long as you can control yourself, we should be all right."

I raised my eyebrows. "As long as *I* can control myself?"

He made sweeping motions with his hands, a smartass smirk shaping his gorgeous lips.

Narrowing my eyes, I scooted to the other side of the bed. He lay on top of the sheets, arranged the pillow under his head, interlaced his fingers over his chest, and closed his eyes.

I admired his profile, as his face relaxed, his lips parting slightly. His strong chest and flat stomach rose and fell. A light dusting of hairs started below his navel and disappeared under the waistband. I had trailed kisses down that path before, and I was tempted to do it now.

But no. I would show him that I could control myself. The question was: could he?

I left the bed and went into the bathroom. I was about to close the door, but I thought fair was fair. I could play his game too. So I left it open a crack. With my back to the door, I took off my clothes and discarded them on the floor. I stood naked in front of the mirror and, in the reflection, caught sight of Jake peering at me. I pulled a nightie from an overnight bag I'd left by the sink and slipped it on. It barely covered my butt and had an open back and spaghetti straps. The front scooped low, and my nipples poked through the thin fabric. I got back into bed and laid next to Jake, facing him. His eyes were wide open now, traversing the length of my body, pausing at my breasts as he licked his lips.

"Sleep tight, Jake," I said, glancing down at the bulging shape in his pants.

I squirmed, trailing my fingers down the sheets and imagining I was caressing his torso. I pressed my thighs together, biting my lower lip, and inhaling his musk.

"Stop, Toni," he said in a growl.

"Um? What are you talking about?"

"You know damn well what I'm talking about."

I turned my back on him, my nightie shifting and climbing up my backside. Jake hissed in a breath, jumped out of bed, and peeling the sheets off the bed, threw them over me.

Glancing back over my shoulder, I said, "Oh, thanks. I was starting to get cold."

"Maybe I'll go sleep on the sofa," he said.

I sobered. "No. Stay. I promise I'll behave."

He thought about it for a moment, then lay back down. For a few beats the sexual tension between us hummed in the air. It passed slowly until we were both breathing rhythmically, allowing sleep to cozy up to us.

Without thinking, I scooted closer and nestled my head in the crook of his arm. We both sighed in contentment and fell asleep together.

CHAPTER 26

The next morning, I arrived at the office in an Uber. All night, I had slept like a baby in Jake's arms, but I was disappointed to find him gone when I woke up. Being next to him was such a comfort, and the memory made me smile from ear to ear.

As I walked up to the agency's door, I found that it was still locked. It was already 8:30 AM, and it was strange not to find Rosalina already there making phone calls and lining up appointments. I unlocked and walked in, checking my cell phone to see if I'd missed any messages, I didn't find anything. I was about to dial her number when I noticed a note on the desk.

"Running a few errands. Will be in around 11 AM," the note read.

Again, I couldn't help but wonder what she was up to and why she wasn't telling me about it. I couldn't blame her. I hadn't been the best of friends lately, nor the best of partners. For all I knew, she was out at a job interview.

Oh, crap! What if that was it? What if she was seeing the writing on the wall and making contingency plans? She was good at those.

"You always have to be prepared, Triple T," she always said.

Witchlights! I needed to get my act together or I might lose her, and what would I do without her? That sounded like a nightmare. I knew I could do this on my own if she decided to leave, but what fun would that be?

"Nope, not going to let that happen," I said, turning on my heel and heading out the door.

I got another Uber, and this time got the driver to take me by The Chained Wolf to pick up my Camaro. I found it right where I'd left it. As I drove past the club entrance, I saw that the broken windows had been boarded up and police tape blocked the door.

Lately, the cops had been dealing with a lot. What had happened at Ulfen's club was not an isolated incident. Skirmishes between werewolves and vampires were not unheard of, but lately they'd been happening more often than not.

The vampire leaders continued to blame the werewolves for rhabo trafficking in the city and killed anyone they found selling the drug on the streets. Recently, they'd switched to bigger targets, though, hence the attack on Ulfen's club. I probably needed to talk to Tom to see what he was doing and tell him what I knew. The poor man might be chasing his tail trying to find a lead on Stephen when we already knew for sure he was behind this.

Twenty-five minutes later, I stopped in front of Damien Ward's house. I sat in my Camaro surveying the sidewalks, searching for a chunk of red hair that might point out Jenson's presence here. I didn't see anything suspicious but didn't let my guard down. Even as I called Mom to check how she was doing, my eyes scanned my surroundings, and my sensitive ears registered every noise.

Mom was doing better, up and about trying to cook. Dani was still hanging out with her to make sure she got enough rest and took her medicine. I promised to go visit her as soon as I could. Dani didn't seem to mind the time off, but it wasn't fair that she should be the only one taking responsibility. I was sure Lucia was no help, and Leo got off scott-free, gallivanting all over South America or who knew where. I hadn't heard from him in a long while, and I was starting to worry. He always emailed at least once a month, but lately it had been nothing but radio silence from him. I needed to check with Dani and Lucia to see if he'd messaged them.

After disconnecting the call, I got out of the car and walked toward the five-story, decrepit-looking building. I stood in front of the door, rang the bell, and waited.

To my surprise, Eric Cross opened the door. He gave me a raised eyebrow and scanned me from head to toe. "You didn't show this morning."

"Hi, good morning to you, too." I put on a smile that showed no teeth.

He continued to stare at me.

"You said I could train with you whenever I wanted."

That didn't erase his scowl either. *What the hell?!* Had he said one thing and meant another? Had he been expecting me to show up every morning at 4 AM?

Aw, maybe he missed me.

Nah, that couldn't be it.

Eric's heart was a lump of ice. He was incapable of missing anyone.

"I was at The Chained Wolf last night," I said.

That did the trick. He let the door swing open and allowed me in.

I stepped into the foyer. "I take it you heard about the brawl that broke out."

"Indeed."

I glanced around the large space and saw that the hidden door at the side of the marble steps was cracked open. "Is Damien down there?"

"Yes. He's doing the final touches on the cure."

"Really?" That got me excited. I would soon have good news for Aaron and Josh. Leaving Eric behind, I headed downstairs into the gloom of the mage's potions room.

Eric came down with me, and we found Damien leaning on his worktable, peering at bubbling flasks in a short-path distillation setup. A blue flame burned steadily under a round flask filled with clear liquid. Glass pipes climbed in different directions, depositing droplets into other instruments. A sweet scent permeated the room, something between honey and burnt caramel.

When he heard us coming down, he glanced away from his concoction and gifted us with his attention.

"I remember saying that I would call you when this was ready," he grumbled.

"Jeez, you two certainly put the grouch in grouchy," I said. "The perfect pair, I suppose."

"She says she was at The Chained Wolf last night," Eric offered.

Damien's cranky expression morphed into one of interest. "What were you doing there?"

"Is there somewhere we can sit and talk? It's a long story. Plus, some weird stuff happened with my abilities, and I was hoping you two could help me understand."

"Weird stuff, huh?" Eric said, then turned to Damien. "You really did a number on her with that spell."

"I've made amends," the mage said. "I brought her to you."

Eric laughed dryly. "I doubt she feels that evens out the score.

Maybe you just built up a bigger debt."

Was that a joke? Was Eric capable of self-deprecating humor? Maybe hell was freezing over.

Damien turned back to his instruments, adjusted the flame that burned under his potion, and nodded to himself. "This should be ready in forty-eight hours."

"That's awesome!" I exclaimed. "I can't wait to give the good news to my client."

The mage turned. "We can talk in the kitchen. I find that my good humor has made me hungry."

Good humor? Seriously? I considered for a moment. Maybe this was what passed for good humor with him. I *had* seen his really awful temper the day he blasted a hole in the floor at my agency, so this was certainly an improvement, and maybe the best I could expect from him.

In the kitchen, Damien went straight to a brand new espresso machine and started fiddling with it, grinding coffee beans and filling the space with their delicious aroma. He pulled a bowl of fruit from the refrigerator and retrieved a box of pastries from a pantry. He laid napkins plates and utensils next to the food and invited us to partake.

I gladly accepted his offerings. My refrigerator was still an echo chamber, and I'd been so intent on getting here that I didn't stop for breakfast. He made a strong cup of coffee for everyone, and provided a little pitcher of heavy cream and a container of sugar cubes that put the "P" in Perfect.

"This is some amazing coffee," I said. "Rosalina would love it."

Damien frowned as I mentioned her name. "How is your friend doing?" he asked, trying too hard to make the question sound casual.

"She's fine," I said. "Worried about our business since we don't have any clients lined up right now. With everything that's going on, it's been kind of hard to operate normally."

"I can imagine." He sipped his coffee then transferred a few pieces of fruit onto his plate and added a Danish from the pastry box.

As I chomped on a strawberry, my eyes darted between the mage and the alpha. They were two unlikely companions—people I would have never met if not for Mom's lies. Yet, I was glad to be here with them, to know them and count them as my friends.

"So, spill," Damien said. "What happened last night?"

I started from the beginning, telling them about Ulfen's visit, and his suspicion that someone was controlling his son through a pendant. Then I told them what had been happening to me when I touched things, how my tracker skills seem to be changing. And about that day I'd sensed Jake's approach.

Finally, I was about to tell them about what I'd seen when I touched Stephen's pendant when I decided that the mention of hybrids might get them too distracted. I wanted to know their opinion about what I'd done to that vampire before they got lost in the weeds of some major conspiracy going on in the city. So I told them about the battle and how I blasted Loud Mouth after turning into a high wattage electric bulb.

Both Eric and Damien remained silent for a moment, staring at me in undisguised surprise.

"So… what's the verdict?" I asked since they remained as mute as bricks. "Am I going to blow up one day when my powers get out of control? Or is this a good thing?"

Eric deferred to Damien, turning his body in the mage's direction and raising his eyebrows.

Damien sighed. "I would be lying if I said I know what's happening to you. All I have are guesses."

"Shoot guesses then."

"Okay, well, maybe my spell kept more than your werewolf in check."

"You mean it also affected my tracking skills?" I asked.

He nodded.

"But trackers can't blast people," I argued.

This time Damien deferred to Eric, who thought for a moment, then said, "The way you bombarded that vampire with your thoughts makes me wonder if you used your alpha powers in combination with your tracking abilities. Maybe, instead of just pushing your thoughts, you also blasted him with a sensory overload. Vampires, like werewolves, have very strong senses, and perhaps, he couldn't handle the force of your mental attack."

All I heard were a lot of "maybes" and "perhaps," which didn't put my mind at ease one bit. I wanted to know when these changes would stop. The onslaught of sensory stimuli might drive me crazy one day.

"I know this is not what you wanted to hear," Eric said, "but the best we can do is keep an eye on you and continue training. Finding out how your skills have evolved while you're in the middle of a battle with a vampire is not optimal. We can push the boundaries while we work together. You better believe that's a much safer method. Don't you think?"

"I guess," I admitted begrudgingly.

Damien was looking at Eric through narrowed eyes as he pensively ran a long index finger over his upper lip. His white eyebrows were raised as he evaluated the werewolf.

"What?" Eric huffed.

"I believe, my dear Eric, that your debt with me is fully repaid. There's no need for you to continue training this young pup." He smiled crookedly, looking satisfied with himself.

"I can't cast her out. Not in her *condition.*" Eric sounded outraged.

"Hey," I protested. "It's not like I'm sick or anything." I frowned. "Am I?"

They both ignored me, and Damien continued his mocking charade. "What difference does it make? People stumble through life every day, completely clueless and helpless."

"Seriously?" I demanded. "I'm not stumbling through life." The words carried no conviction. Considering the craziness of the last few weeks, there definitely had been a lot of stumbling.

"Somebody's got to do something," Eric argued. "Since the guilty party," he stared pointedly at the mage, "is washing his hands of her."

Damien looked to the heavens with a dramatic flair. "Oh, Eric, why don't you just admit it? You have taken a liking to Toni."

Eric crossed his arms and glowered, closing himself off, refusing to answer Damien's question.

"It seems to me that thou protests too much." Damien chuckled.

Exasperated, Eric threw his arms up in the air and abandoned his stool. "And what if I have?"

I peered at Eric's scowling face, trying to see past his hardened exterior. Did he truly like me? Had he opened up his heart to let me in? It seemed he had been closed off for years, and with good reason. The pain he must have experienced when he lost his family was unimaginable. I'd nearly lost Mom this week, and it had been enough to make me forget all my resentment and start a clean slate between us. Family was everything, and I would be crippled without them.

"Perhaps, she reminds me of someone," Eric said, as if he needed an excuse to like me.

"Bravo." Damien started slow clapping like a prissy lady at the opera. "The tough and unmovable Eric Lone has found his heart."

Really? Could Damien be any more insensitive. At this rate, he was going to send Eric's heart back into hiding.

Time for a bomb that would stop all this nonsense. "Ulfen thinks someone is trying to create a hybrid pack."

Eric and Damien fainted.

No, not really, but they did turn pale as ghosts and forgot all about their banter.

I had their attention again.

CHAPTER 27

I could read their expressions like a road sign. Damien and Eric knew exactly what I meant by "hybrid pack." As I explained what I had seen in my vision, I learned that they'd heard of the Unholy Vessel, and that, like Ulfen's ancestors, Eric's had also been involved in hunting down the bloodthirsty monsters after the mage was done with them.

"We have to find out more," Eric said after I'd laid out all the cards on the table. "We need to get our hands on that pendant."

"How?" I asked.

Eric looked at me as if I was stupid and he regretted liking me, whether or not I reminded him of someone.

I vaguely wondered who. His daughter, perhaps? Hopefully not his wife because that would be weird. I shook the thought away, refusing to give it credit.

"It's simple, Sunder," Eric said. "We take it from Stephen. I don't know why Ulfen hasn't simply done that. This is serious. If his son is, in any way, trying to create hybrids, he has to stop him. Hybrids are vile monsters. They have no respect for life. All they care about is blood and destruction. A sufficient number of them could raze the city to the ground in no time."

I pushed away my empty cup of coffee as my stomach did a somersault that left me feeling nauseous. "But what if someone is controlling him like Ulfen believes? What if none of it is Stephen's fault? I know him, and I don't think he's the kind of person who would come up with a crazy plot like this. If we openly confront him, we would lose our advantage. But if we lay low, he might lead us to the real culprit before they start creating hybrids."

"She has a point," Damien said.

Eric huffed. "What if they've already started creating them?"

"We don't know that," I said.

"Then what do you suggest we do?"

"We could… follow Stephen," I said. "See if he leads us to someone or to the Unholy Vessel."

"That might turn out to be a big waste of time," Damien said. "I doubt the mage who's controlling him would make a mistake like that."

I didn't point out that a witch, and not a mage, could be responsible. There was no way to be sure, except…

"Do you think Jenson Boyle is powerful enough for something like this?" I asked. "Could he be the one trying to create the hybrids? He seems power hungry to me."

So far, I'd been thinking of Jenson as an accomplice, someone beneath Stephen in the pecking order, but what if that wasn't the case? What if this was all his doing?

Damien nodded, if a bit reluctantly. "He's a Copper Mage now, so yes, he could be the one controlling Erickson. But he's not the brightest bulb in the box. He's been a laughing stock in our circles since he appeared on the scene some years back. He has ambition, sure, but not the smarts to come up with a scheme like this."

"How about some of the other pack leaders. Craig Blackridge? Walter Knight?" I hated to bring Jake's grandfather up, but he struck me as the ruthless, manipulative kind. Hesitantly, I added one more name, "Travis Hillworth?"

Eric and Damien exchanged a glance.

"I know he's my father." I shrugged. "I asked my mother, and she told me."

After considering for a moment, Eric spoke. "I could be wrong, but I don't think any werewolf in their right mind would turn another one into a hybrid. The St. Louis packs may not always get along, but they have learned to live in relative harmony. The local packs are doing well. Why would they try to upset the balance?"

"The vampires then. Bernadetta Fiore, her driver was there the day we found Stephen. Though that would mean she's responsible for rhabo and killing many of her own kind."

"Bernadetta Fiore would kill her own mother for a pittance if it gave her another gram of power," Eric said. "Though, if she's involved, I'd like to know how she found out about the Unholy Vessel. Its existence is only known by a few packs whose ancestors made a pact to protect the secret."

Gah! My head hurt just thinking about all the possibilities.

I hopped off the stool. "I guess I'd better get back to the office. Will you call me when the cure is ready?" I asked Damien.

He answered with a simple nod. I couldn't wait to surprise Aaron and Josh with the good news.

ഇരു

When I got back to the office, I found Rosalina sitting at her desk, typing away at the computer. Her cheeks were flushed, and her makeup wasn't as perfect as usual. I sat across from her, frowning.

"Where were you?" I asked.

"Oh, just running around," she said, waving a hand in the air and never meeting my gaze. "My abuelita needed me to buy a few things for her. What about you?"

I told her what had happened at The Chained Wolf. She abandoned the computer to listen, her eyes getting wider and wider as I went on. When I was done, her surprise had morphed into something close to anger, though.

"I'm glad Jake was there," she said. "I never figured Stephen for a coward. And these new powers of yours, what if they hadn't showed up in time? You would be dead."

I winced at that. She wasn't wrong. Loud Mouth would've taken my head off and played football with it.

"You got lucky, Toni. Admit it."

"I know I did."

I waited for her to get started on me, telling me that I was taking too many risks, that I would get myself killed. But she didn't. Instead, she took a deep breath to calm herself and changed the topic of conversation.

"I think I have someone lined up who will sign a contract today." She hit a few keys on her keyboard, and the printer came to life. "He's not a high-profile client, more of a mid-list one, but better than nothing. If we book him, we'll almost have enough to pay all our bills without touching our savings."

"Sounds good!" I took the newly printed papers and looked them over. "Thanks for doing this."

She shrugged.

"Oh, I forgot to mention… Damien's cure should be ready soon. I can't wait to give it to Aaron and Josh. It must be nerve-racking, going through that. And not to sound self-centered, but maybe once Josh is better, having a famous DJ in our customer base will begin to pay off."

"Hopefully." She didn't sound convinced, and I didn't feel too confident about it either. We had put Aaron through a very painful situation. It was unlikely that he would take a risk by sending any of his close friends our way.

We set to work, getting ready for the new customer's arrival later that afternoon. When he arrived, we talked in my office. He was in his mid-thirties and had gone through an ugly divorce a couple of years ago. He wished to start a family and wasn't willing to take that leap with just anyone. This time, he wanted to make sure he found someone compatible who shared his views and family values. His parents had divorced when he was little, and he didn't want to put his own children through that.

He sounded like a great guy, just the kind of person I liked to help. He did most of the talking while I listened, and in the end, he didn't take much convincing to get on board and sign our contract. He was just ready to begin a new stage in his life. I breathed more at ease after he left, knowing that we would be able to pay our bills if I found him a mate.

At the end of the day, I followed Rosalina to her condo and packed a few boxes in the trunk of my Camaro. I made sure to get all my bathroom necessities and some clothes, which was what I'd been missing the most. I'd hoped to hang out with her for a bit, but she said she had somewhere to be and sent me on my way.

She'd really been busy lately, and I couldn't help but wonder if I had cramped her style all those times I'd stayed with her. Maybe she spent a lot more time with her family than I'd realized. Maybe she had a secret life of wild parties or as a scrapbooking aficionado. Who knew?

I headed home, my head spinning with a million thoughts. I

tried not to worry about the agency, reassuring myself that we were back on track with this new customer. I told myself to be patient and that tomorrow the rhabo cure would be ready and Josh would be all right.

I also reasoned that this whole hybrid situation was not my responsibility. I was just a tracker, recently turned werewolf, who had gotten pulled into an impossible shitstorm. The best I could do was stay out of it, and let the packs sort out their own mess. I had my own life to live, my own friends and family to worry about. I didn't want bad things happening in my city, but I couldn't carry the weight of such responsibility on my shoulders.

I was only one lone wolf, after all.

Finding some measure of comfort in my thoughts, I pulled into my parking space and shut off the engine. I exhaled a heavy sigh. I'd come up with a few convincing arguments to keep myself out of trouble, right?

Yep. You go, Toni! Keep it up and you might actually believe it.

Chuckling, I got out of the Camaro and popped the trunk open. I stacked two boxes on top of each other and headed toward the elevator. I was almost there when steps echoed behind me. As I started to glance back over my shoulder, the steps quickened.

My instincts flared, sensing a threat. I dropped the boxes and whirled around. Someone rammed into me, tackling me to the ground. I hit the pavement hard, my bones rattling. I blinked up at my attacker to discover it was Stephen Erickson.

He hopped on top of me, a fist pulled back. I raised my arms to cover my face, but he was too fast and, before I could protect myself, his fist slammed against the side of my face, and everything went black.

CHAPTER 28

I awoke in stages. I was sitting, my head lolling. My temples pounded, and my jaw felt stiff and hurt like someone had hit it with a hammer. I opened my eyes, blinking at the dim, warm light that surrounded me. Flickering candles sat on top of what looked like a marble altar. A wooden crucifix with a life-sized Jesus hung upside down on the wall. Stained-glass windows with five-pointed pentagrams lined either side of the cross. A sturdy wooden lectern sat off to one side.

What the hell?!

I glanced around, wincing at the pain as I moved my neck.

Pews lined up to my right and left. I was in the middle aisle, my hands and legs tied to a chair. Clearly, I was in some sort of church, though not a traditional one.

The smell of burnt candles wafted through the air. I listened for any sounds but heard nothing. It seemed I was alone. I strained to see behind me where the exit must be, but I perceived only shadows.

Gritting my teeth, I strained against my bonds. They were tight and bit into my wrists and ankles. I wondered what would happen if I shifted, would they still hold me? If they did, I would've at least gained sharp teeth to rip through the rope. There was only one way to find out.

I called on my wolf, inviting her forward.

Nothing happened.

I tried again.

Nothing.

Panic set in. What was happening?

"Shifting won't work here," Stephen's voice said behind me.

I froze.

My nose twitched, trying to detect his scent, but I got nothing. He was probably wearing some of that ScentKill stuff Jake owned, just the reason I hadn't sensed him coming in the parking lot.

"There are spells on coven temples that work against shifters. Pretty powerful, huh?"

Coven temples? I was in a freaking vampire church? What the hell? My mind raced. My heart did too.

Steps sounded behind me, tapping on the stone floor, approaching at an excruciatingly slow pace. A shiver ran up my spine as I waited, expecting him to punch me again. But he simply ambled by, his hand caressing my arm as he passed. Then he stepped in front of me and regarded me quietly for a long time. He wore a gray suit with a white shirt, but no tie.

He reached for my face. "Sorry I had to hit you. Does it hurt too much?"

I yanked my chin out of his grip, sneering, itching to return the favor, picturing my fist slamming across his perfect jaw, imagining his teeth falling out one by one.

"What is this?!" I demanded. "Why?"

"You know well why. Let's stop pretending. Your meddling is

getting old, Toni. I was willing to let you be despite all the trouble you caused in the warehouse." He shook his head, putting on a sad expression. "You almost killed Blake, and you almost cost us one thousand pounds of rhabo."

Almost definitely applied to Blake but not the rhabo.

"The police seized the entire shipment," I said. "What the hell are you talking about?"

He laughed and lazily walked in a circle. "We have so many cops in our pockets it's not even funny. When they sent the drug to be destroyed, we simply got it back."

Oh, no! My heart sank. How many more would die? All of our efforts have been in vain. My eyes filled with tears as the blow of our failure hit me.

Stephen gave me a creepy smile. "I like you, Toni. A lot. Too much, maybe."

His blue eyes scanned the length of my body with a hunger I didn't like at all. My stomach roiled in disgust. This was not the Stephen I knew, not at all. I had never heard him talk this way. He sounded slimy and perverted. Was somebody else talking through him? Or was this really him and I'd been completely deluded?

"And now that I know you're a werewolf, you're even more tempting than before." He inhaled deeply. "You smell delicious." He licked his lips.

I fought against my bindings, wishing I could get a leg free to kick him in the balls. Still, maybe I should give him the benefit of the doubt.

"Who gave you that pendant you wear, Stephen?"

He frowned, looking at me as if I were stupid. "What does that matter?" A pause. "Look, I brought you here because I want to discuss something with you."

"Oh, yeah? Do you make a habit of tying people up when you

want to talk to them?"

"I knew you were on to me. You wouldn't have come." He said this as if it were the perfect excuse for abducting people.

"I risked my life for you," I said. "I thought you were in danger, but your kidnapping was all a sham. Why would you do something like that?"

He narrowed his eyes. "I know you must have a lot of questions, and since I'm willing to play nice I will answer them gladly. Shoot."

I froze for a moment, overwhelmed by all the thoughts bouncing around in my head. Shaking myself, I decided to start from the beginning.

"Did you fake your own kidnapping?"

"Yes. It was quite fun." He grinned like a maniac.

"Did you send people to hurt me?

"Oh, no. They weren't going to hurt you. They were only supposed to scare you, get you fired up about finding me. I knew Jake would be, but I wanted *you* to find me."

"Why?"

He ran a finger along the arm of one of the pews and rubbed the dust between his fingers. "My rescue needed to appear convincing and involving you lent the whole affair credibility, especially with the likes of Tom Freeman."

"How did you disguise your wolf when that Copper Mage attacked us at the restaurant?"

"That?" He pulled a face as if this question was a waste of time. "That was just a stupid little spell from Jenson. I couldn't have Jake recognize me. I regret not killing him that night, but I didn't think he would become such a pain in the ass. It had all worked out great, though."

"Meaning you got your father in jail."

Stephen nodded and grinned again.

"Why? He cares about you."

He shrugged as if that made no difference. "He's mediocre and content with a small slice of a very big pie. He bores me."

I opened my mouth to ask another question, but he waved a hand in the air. "This bores me, too. Enough questions." He narrowed his eyes and leaned forward, bringing his nose close to mine. "Join my pack, Toni."

I almost choked. Was he for real? Join his pack? I would rather birth a barbed-wire bat. My first instinct was to spit on his face, but was that smart? Something told me he wouldn't just give me a pat on the back and let me go.

"Why would I do that?" I asked, attempting to buy myself time as I tried to figure out a way out of this bind.

"I'm glad you asked." He angled my chair toward one of the pews. The sound of wood scraping against stone echoed through the temple. He sat and crossed his legs. "There are many good reasons. For one, you don't want to be a lone wolf. You need a pack, trust me. A beautiful, young werewolf like you… someone will try to snatch you up." He chuckled. "I guess someone already did."

The bastard thought this was funny. My wolf stirred inside of me, roiling with anger. I tried to call her forward again, but nothing happened. My skin didn't even itch.

"I would protect you," he went on. "No one would dare lay a finger on you. Soon, my pack will be more powerful than all the St. Louis packs combined. You could be part of that. You could be at my side, enjoying the power and luxury. No more scraping for a few dollars at your little *agency*."

He pronounced the last word as if he were talking about garbage, and that made my anger redouble. *Gah!* When I got free, I would send him packing to jail, though not before I nailed him by the balls to the apex of The Gateway Arch.

"Is that all?" I asked. "Or do you have any more bullet points to present?"

His expression hardened. He pushed to the edge of the pew, his eyes drilling into mine. "I sense you're mocking me."

Boy, he's perceptive.

"I only ask because I need to know everything before I make such an important decision, don't you think?"

He grunted.

"For instance, when you say 'your pack,' do you mean your father's pack? Or an entirely new one?"

"My father's pack is a joke."

I nodded. "Okay, so a new pack. How many are there? What if I don't like them? Maybe I should meet them first."

"Quit fucking with me." He stood in one swift motion, grabbed me by the neck, and squeezed until I could hardly breathe. "This is no joke. I've been patient with you. I've forgiven your interference, but I won't be lenient for much longer."

I struggled to take in air, my lungs beginning to burn, my wolf thrashing, fighting to get out but running into some invisible wall every time she made an attempt.

Finally, he let me go, shoving my face to one side as he took a step back. I took several gulps of air, wincing at the pain in my windpipe, willing my woozy head to clear.

"Okay," I coughed. "I'll do whatever you want."

"You're lying," he spat, kicking at my chair, right between my thighs.

The legs scraped against the stone floor as the chair skidded backwards, then it caught on something and the front legs rose in the air. I teetered for a second and tried to throw my weight forward, but crashed to the floor all the same. The back of my head hit stone. White stars exploded in my vision. I growled between my teeth as pain thrilled down my spine. My vision blurred, and I took deep breaths and blinked rapidly, fighting hard not to lose consciousness.

I focused on the exposed wooden beams in the high ceiling, then turned my head from side to side, taking deep breaths. I blinked at a thick marble column to my right, at the gray veins that spidered through its smooth surface.

Stay awake, Toni. Stay awake!

Stephen reached for the chair and pulled it back up. The whole temple seemed to spin for a moment but slowly came to a stop.

He squatted in front of me and caressed my chin, his anger gone and replaced by a sweet smile. "I know it won't be that easy to convince you, Toni. You're strong and stubborn, and I like that about you. But I also know that when you come around, you'll be loyal to me—the way you are loyal to Jake." His smile disappeared. "He doesn't love you. He's marrying someone else for power. That's where he and I are different. You see," he straightened and stretched his arms over his head, "I'm doing it all on my own. Building my own pack. I don't need my father. I don't need to marry someone to gain strength. I'm strong all on my own, and I'm choosing you, even though you have nothing to offer."

Gee, thanks. He was a total charmer, knew just how to make a girl feel appreciated.

"Jake has no real ambition," he went on, turning his back on me and pacing away. "He wants to work as a stupid private eye." He laughed. "He might one day be a pack leader, but only because his dead father and his clever, manipulative grandfather have more ambition than he does." He stopped, his eyes raised toward the stained-glass windows at the back of the altar.

I glanced sideways at the marble column. It was only a few feet away. I wrapped my hands around the curved arms of the chair. I had an idea, but I would only get one chance, so I had to make it count.

With a deep breath, as if to gather resolve out of the air, I rocked forward and onto my feet. Stephen whirled and stared at me with a frown. I must've looked ridiculous, hunched over and with the chair sticking to my backside like some albatross.

He cocked his head sideways.

Shit!

Not time to waste.

I ran sideways and smashed the chair against the column with all my might just as he rushed in my direction. There was a loud crack and the albatross at my back went wonky. I tried to get free, but it wasn't enough. I took a step back and ran at the column again. I crashed into it a second time… another crack accompanied by a splintering sound.

Stephen reached me, grabbed me by the shoulders, and forced me down. The chair legs settled on the floor, and for a moment, I thought it hadn't worked, but as my full weight rested on the chair, it fell to bits and I collapsed onto a pile of broken pieces.

Thrashing with my arms and legs, I came free of the bulk of the chair, though parts of it clung to me still attached by the ropes. Stephen came at me, trying to hold me down, but I kicked at him from my prone position, keeping him away as I struggled to undo the ropes.

"You don't need to fight me," he grunted as, once more, he tried to take hold of my legs and I kicked his hands away. "I'm asking you to be on my side."

I freed one of my legs of its wooden appendage, then the other. Scrambling, I got to my feet. The arms of the chair still clung to me as I backed away from Stephen. I clumsily, desperately, worked at the ropes around my left wrist and got it loose. The armrest *thunked* to the floor. Getting the other one off was easier, and I decided to keep it as a weapon.

I pointed the splintered piece of wood at Stephen. "Stay away from me, you bastard or I swear I will kill you."

I backed away toward the double doors ready to escape.

CHAPTER 29

Stephen smirked, peering at my makeshift weapon with contempt. Then, he came at me, moving so fast that I had no time to even raise the broken piece of wood. He crashed into me, wrapping his arms around my waist and knocking me to the floor. The armrest slipped from my hand and clattered under one of the pews. Air *whooshed* out of my mouth as the impact crushed my abdomen and lungs.

Just like he'd done in the parking lot, Stephen straddled me, pinning me down. He tried to take hold of my arms, but I fought him, slapping and clawing at him. As he leaned over me, I caught a glimpse of the chain at his neck. On a reflex, I went for it and managed to take hold of it. A rainbow of colors flashed before my eyes. Blinded, I pulled on the chain, trying to tear it off him.

His eyes opened wide in panic, and he tilted further down toward me, releasing the tension on the chain. I doubled down, wrapping more of the chain around my fingers until it was taut again. I yanked as hard as I could. The chain bit into Stephen's neck. He grabbed my wrist, tried to hold it in place so I couldn't pull anymore.

With his attention focused on saving his little relic, I called on my self-defense training and nudged him off balance by slamming my knees into his backside. He lurched sideways, bracing an arm against the floor to avoid falling. It was all I needed to worm my way out from under him. In one fluid motion, I flipped on my side, curled my legs up, pressed my feet against his hips, and kicked while pulling on the chain.

The thing finally broke. The heavy pendant slid down the length of the chain and *clanked* to the floor. It had a bulky, orange jewel set in a silver base. Stephen let go of my wrist. I scrambled away and jumped to my feet, struggling with my need to breathe. He stayed on the floor, staring at the pendant as if in a trance.

Slowly, he knelt, his shoulders drooping, his chin on his chest as he stared at the glittering stone. As if waking up from a dream, he blinked up and looked at me.

"Toni?" he said, seeming surprised to find me there. He glanced around the temple, frowning. "What… what's going on?"

I kept my distance, my heart pounding, mind racing, and lungs finally refilling.

Shakily, holding onto one of the pews, Stephen pushed himself up and stood. He rubbed the side of his neck where an angry red mark beaded with tiny droplets of blood.

He sucked air through his teeth. "That burns." His blue eyes met mine again. "Why are we here?"

"Y-you don't remember?"

He shook his head.

"Let's go," I urged. "I'll explain later."

He nodded, looking unsure.

I headed for the double doors and tried to push them open. They didn't budge. I pulled on them. Nothing. Glancing over my shoulder, I said, "Help me op—"

Stephen wrapped an arm around my neck and put me in a chokehold. "You're so gullible, Toni," he said in my ear as he pulled me away from the exit.

I clawed at his arm and kicked as my feet dragged down the aisle, the doors stretching further away. Bucking like a wild horse, I growled. Frustration washed over me. I was so stupid. So stupid.

"One way or another, you'll be with me," he whispered in my ear, his breath hot and disgustingly wet.

Suddenly, the doors clanked open , and several figures appeared under the arched entrance, dark shapes silhouetted by a dim light from outside.

"Help!" I screamed, but the figures remained still for a long moment, then finally started marching down the aisle.

Steps echoed on the stone floor. Someone led what looked like a procession, two lines of people walking in pairs. When the glow of candlelight finally illuminated the line leader, my breath caught.

It was Bernadetta Fiore, advancing toward us as if she were floating on air. She wore a black bodysuit that hugged her petite figure like a second skin. A trench coat, a leather corset, and knee-high boots with metal buckles and heels as sharp as knives completed the outfit. Her jet black hair was pulled tight against her scalp, ending in a high ponytail held in place by a thick gold band. Her dark gaze was cool and detached.

A thrill of fear raked across my back. We had been right from the beginning. The Dark Donna was behind all of this, but I would've never imagined Stephen becoming her ally. This explained Bertram's presence that night at the repair shop where we found the Lucciola van, and why the vampire hadn't hurt me. Probably, Stephen had told him not to.

Ten vampires—their faces pale, their eyes lined with dark

veins—walked in two lines to her right and left. They each pushed someone along, keeping their clawed hands at their captives' necks, forcing them forward. My nose twitched. The captives were werewolves. Their scent was unmistakable. A dark-skinned vamp dressed all in red leather was impossible to miss standing to Bernadetta's right, a cloud of bleached blond hair framing her face.

Oh, shit! Was this what I thought it was?

Bernadetta stopped in front of us. Air wheezed through my throat, struggling with Stephen's relentless chokehold.

"I take it you couldn't convince her," Bernadetta said, enunciating each word with her careful way of talking.

"She's spirited," Stephen said with amusement in his tone. "It's one of the many things I love about her."

The vamp nodded. "Yes, she doesn't intimidate easily." Her deep black eyes assessed me carefully. "I tried to warn you to stay away, Ms. Sunder."

"You lied," I spat.

"Did I?" She raised her manicured eyebrows. "I told you I hadn't kidnapped Stephen, and it was true. He was a willing participant."

"Don't play stupid. You were behind it all along."

The vamp rushed me in a blur of movement and, bearing her pointed fangs, hissed in my face. "Talk to me like that one more time, and I will pluck your little eyes out." She raised a fist, then her claw-tipped index finger sprang up like a switchblade.

"She will behave," Stephen said behind me. "Won't you, Toni?" His tone was conciliatory and made me realize he took Bernadetta's threats seriously. "Besides, in a few minutes, she will be nothing but obedient."

No. No!

Renewing my struggle, I slammed and elbow into Stephen's

ribs. He *humphed* but didn't loosen his hold.

I had to get free. They had the Unholy Vessel, and they meant to use it on me and on the other werewolves they'd brought. Once more, I called my wolf forward, willing her to manifest with all my might. I felt her under the surface, fighting to come forward, but it was useless.

Desperately, I glanced over at the captives, searching their faces. A few of them wore strained expressions as if they were trying to call on their wolves, too. Others simply appeared resigned and kept their heads low, eyes to the floor.

This was it. Without being able to shift, we couldn't fight. We were stronger than Stales even in our human forms, but not as strong as vampires—not unless we shifted. But this place…

I glanced around, hopelessness flooding my heart.

Bernadetta climbed the three steps to the altar and faced us. A cold, little smile stretched her lips. She reached into her trench coat and pulled something out: a cylindrical container that appeared to be made out of jade. It was no bigger than a soda can, with a handle of the same polished, green material, protruding from the top. It had to be the Unholy Vessel.

The vamp delicately set the object on the marble altar, then pulled on the top piece. A small dagger slid out, its silver edge reflecting the candlelight. Without preamble, she positioned her hand over the vessel and used the dagger to slice her palm open.

An angry, red gash gaped open. She made a fist, squeezing hard, and a thin stream of blood trickled into the jade cup, through the narrow slit where the dagger had rested. The wound closed within seconds, and the vamp used the dagger again to make another cut. She had to cut herself one more time and, after checking the vessel to make sure it was filled to satisfaction, she ran her tongue over her palm, lapping up the blood that remained after the wound closed for the third time. Bile rose in my throat as her pink tongue flicked in and out, her hooded eyes set on Stephen.

When she was done, she gestured toward me. "Bring her here."

"One of the other ones first," Stephen said. "Just to make sure."

The Dark Donna shrugged and glanced toward the vampire dressed in red leather. She pushed her captive werewolf forward, a young man in his early twenties, no more than a few years older than me. He was struggling against his captor, but she manhandled him as if the werewolf were no more than a child. She practically carried him up the steps and placed him in front of Bernadetta.

"Don't touch me," he growled at the petite vampiress.

He was a head taller than Bernadetta, but her powerful aura made her seem greater than life.

"Worry not," she smirked. "I won't lay a finger on you. I avoid touching your kind like the plague. I hate the stench." She turned, picked up the dagger from the altar, and stuck it inside the vessel. "One drop will do," she said in a musical tone as she pulled the dagger back out. The silver blade was covered with a sheen of blood. She held it steady for a bit as droplets of her blood splashed back into the jade cup.

Grinning with satisfaction, a glint in her eyes, she faced the werewolf and gestured toward the red-clad vamp. "Open his mouth, Danika."

The werewolf struggled, shaking his head, trying to get free, but Danika forced him to his knees, and, with one hand, squeezed his face until his lips parted open.

"Stop!" I cried out, but no one paid me any mind.

Bernadetta tiptoed closer, holding the dagger in front of her, inching it closer toward the werewolf's mouth. He screamed, hopelessly fighting against the arms that held him in place, his legs thrashing as the rest of his body was kept in place.

The blade hovered over the werewolf's lips. A drop of blood quivered at the tip of the blade. The werewolf's face disfigured in terror.

I fought against Stephen. "Let him go, you psychopaths. Stephen, don't do this. If you do this, there's no coming back from it."

The drop of blood fell. For a second, it seemed to hover frozen in midair. I thought of a miracle that might stop it, but the drop plunged into the man's opened mouth, sizzling on contact. The hands that held him released him.

The man dropped to all fours, sputtering and spitting. Bernadetta took a couple of steps back, her head cocked to one side as she regarded him with curiosity.

He slowly rose to his feet and glanced around, chest heaving, hatred burning in his gaze.

"You'll pay for this." He reached for Bernadetta, wrapping his hands around her neck.

She didn't even flinch. Danika made as if to pull the man back, but the Dark Donna waved her back. In the next instant, the man began trembling all over. He tried to hold onto the vamp, but he fell to the floor and flopped like a fish out of water. He clawed at his throat, screaming and arching his back to the breaking point. A blue light shone under his skin, descending from his throat to the rest of his body and also climbing to the top of his head.

"Fascinating," Bernadetta observed as the man continued to thrash, crying out in agony.

I wanted to turn away, to close my eyes so I wouldn't have to see his suffering, so I wouldn't have to witness what would happen to me next, but I was transfixed.

Suddenly, the man went utterly still, his cries turning into soft moans. At last, he went silent. Was he dead?

Maybe something had gone wrong, or I should say… something had gone terribly right? Because I would rather die than become the Dark Donna's mind slave.

Bernadetta exchanged a glance with Stephen. It seemed she also thought something had gone wrong. She opened her mouth to say something when the man twitched and sat up straight with a jolt.

The Dark Donna made an approving sound in the back of her throat. "Stand," she ordered.

The man rose to his feet and faced her, looking like a soldier ready for his next command.

"Act like a monkey," she ordered.

The man placed one hand on top of his head and the other on his butt and started scratching both places simultaneously while he walked around with bent knees saying, "Ooh, ooh, ooh, ah, ah."

Bernadetta laughed and her vampires laughed with her, looking delighted.

"This is easier than compulsion," she said. "Totally effortless."

"Ooh, ooh, ooh, ah, ah." The man seemed to be getting carried away and started bouncing up and down on the balls of his feet and beating his chest.

"Enough," the vamp said.

He stopped, straightened his back, and waited for his next command.

"Stand aside and wait."

The man retreated, bowing his head respectfully and standing with his hands behind his back.

Bernadetta turned to Stephen. "She's next."

I dug my heels in. "No, please don't let her do that to me."

This couldn't happening. Stephen pushed me forward.

"No!" I cried out. "Please. I'll be on your side, Stephen." I would say anything to stop them from feeding me that poison.

"You had your chance," Stephen said. "If you had simply considered it, I would have given you the opportunity to prove yourself."

Danika grabbed my arms and forced me to my knees. She took a handful of my hair and pulled my head back. Bernadetta dipped the dagger into the vessel once more and approached me. Her expression told me how pleased she felt to find me kneeling in front of her, ready to become her slave.

Digging in her claws, Danika grabbed my face and squeezed. I clenched my teeth together with all my might, but her fingers painfully dug into the hollows of my cheeks, slowly prying my mouth open.

Bernadetta placed the dagger over my mouth. A drop of blood slid to the tip and hung there for a split second. Then it fell, ready to seal my fate and give my life over to the evil vamp.

CHAPTER 30

I closed my eyes, despair washing over me as I thought of my family and friends. They would be as lost to me as my life.

I waited for the drop to hit my tongue, for a bitter taste to fill my mouth. Two beats. Nothing. I opened my eyes and stared incredulously at the hovering droplet of blood.

It hung frozen in midair.

A miracle *had* happened.

Bernadetta was staring at me, still smiling coldly. She hadn't noticed the blood was hovering in place. It took her another split second to see what was happening. She frowned, took a step to one side for a better angle, and stared at the blood.

"What—?"

A ball of magic hit her in the chest and sent her flying against the marble altar. The top cleaved in two, rumbling as it collapsed. Shots rang at the entrance. Bullets pinged against the walls. The hands that held me let go. I threw my arms over my head and crawled around the lectern. Stephen joined me, nearly knocking me out of cover. I cursed at him.

Steps rushed over the stone floor. Wood splintered as more shots hit the pews. Another ball of magic flew in and hit one of the stained-glass windows above the altar. I expected them to shatter, but the magic flew past them like a fiery ghost. This place's spells had spells, I imagined.

Bernadetta rose from the ground in one smooth motion, her trench coat fluttering behind her as she hovered above the broken pieces of marble, literally levitating.

Holy shit!

I'd heard ancient vampires could do that, but I always thought it was bullshit.

Suddenly, Stephen lunged toward the broken altar. I watched as he scooped the jade cup from a puddle of blood in the floor and cradled it against his chest. Next, his eyes darted around, searching for the dagger. I spotted it an instant before he did and dove for it. I snatched it up just as Stephen crashed into me and tried to pry it from my fingers. I whirled to a kneeling position and threatened to stab him with it. The blade was still covered in Bernadetta's blood. He recoiled, terror brimming in his eyes.

I had a mind to stick it in his mouth so he could taste a bit of his own medicine, but a bullet flew an inch in front of my nose, and I had to duck and crawl behind one of the marble columns. From that vantage point, I was finally able to see what was happening. The temple was a war zone. Vampires blurred in a flurry of movement, trying to reach the double doors as bullets and magic poured in keeping them at bay. Something told me that if those doors closed, we were all doomed. This was some strange temple, probably soaked in layers and layers of spells.

"Close the doors," Bernadetta ordered in a booming voice too strong for someone so little. She still hovered over the broken altar, her eyes glowing red, her black ponytail fluttering as if a storm were stirring around her.

Another magical attack flew in her direction. Before it reached her, she dropped to the floor and ran toward the doors in a zigzag pattern, blurring with speed. Danika reached the front a second later. They each pushed on one of the thick doors as if they were made of cardboard. The doors swung out, but just before they shut, a current of magic slipped through the crack and, like flooding water, glided over the floor, and spread until it reached every corner of the chamber.

I stared as the magic glowed under my feet, and suddenly my wolf stirred with power, making me realize I was free to shift. I almost did, except I was holding onto the jade dagger and didn't want to let it go.

The captive werewolves, which up to this point had been defenseless, all shifted without hesitation. The bravest of them immediately jumped to attack their captors. Two identical, black werewolves leaped in unison at one of the vampires, taking him by surprise. They ripped his head clean off. Not content with that, they proceeded to rip him up limb by limb, their jaws snapping and breaking what sounded like stone.

Another blast of magic came through the front doors and ripped one of them off its hinges. The massive door flew across the chamber, flipping and spinning, then slammed against a vampire and crushed her against the wall.

A massive werewolf rushed in through the arched entryway, taking a leap and smashing into Danika.

Jake!

How had he found me?

Eric's wolf rushed in on Jake's heels, followed by Damien. The mage wore his top hat and cloak and marched in with confidence. His hands weaved at a prodigious speed as he shot spells right and left, hitting those vampires who weren't fast enough to get out of the way.

My wolf was bursting to get out and join them in the fight. I peered around and spotted a basin on a pedestal, the kind that Catholic churches use for holy water. I had no idea what they could use it for in a place like this, but it would serve as a hiding place. Quickly, I searched for Stephen but couldn't see him anywhere. I left my hiding spot, ran towards the basin, and surreptitiously dropped the jade dagger inside.

In the same motion, I shifted, reveling in the transformation of my body as my muscles grew and hardened, claws tore from my fingertips, and fangs elongated in my mouth. My clothes tore and dropped to the floor. Relishing the strength in my limbs, I leaped forward, landed on top of a vampire, and raked my claws across his back.

The creature howled in pain. I clamped my jaws around his neck and twisted my body to one side, using my momentum. There was a crack. He windmilled his arms, trying to hit me. I released him and landed a few feet away. He swayed on his feet, his head lopsided and his neck gaping. Eyes wide with panic, he righted his head, and the wound started healing right before my eyes.

Oh, no, you don't.

I attacked again, jumping over a pew and propelling forward. My front paws collided with his chest, ripping through his shirt and digging into hard flesh. Reaching out, he held me back just in time. My jaws snapped shut an inch from his face.

Pain stabbed into my shoulders as he sank his claws in. I pushed against his stomach with my hind legs and shook myself free. My back hit the floor. Stumbling, I righted myself and was going in for a second attack when I noticed movement out of the corner of my eye.

Jake was still fighting Danika, and a second vampire was rushing him behind. I pivoted, changing directions, and, realizing that I wouldn't get there in time, rammed my body against the corner of the nearest pew, causing it to fan out on the other end and clip the vampire at the legs. He tripped and sprawled on the floor. The crash drew Jake's attention, letting him know of his sneaking opponent. He immediately spun, clamped his jaw around his neck, and snapped it in two.

These bastards didn't fight fair. If they did, they wouldn't stand a chance against us.

I returned my attention to my opponent, my rage mounting. He had picked up a jagged piece of wood and was rushing in my direction. I dodged. His stake missed me by mere inches. The vamp skidded to a stop and whirled, holding the piece of wood like a bat and swinging at me. I ducked, crouching low on all fours, then as soon as the blow whistled over my head, I jumped forward, clamped my teeth around his ankle, and severed his foot.

He lost his balance and fell, but quickly sprang to a sitting position. As I prepared to attack again, a shot hit him right in the heart, and he slumped backward, holding his chest.

I blinked and stared at his fallen body for several beats. He looked dead, but I have no way of knowing whether or not he really was—no breath or heartbeat to listen for. The sounds of battle raged around me. A pew flew overhead and smashed against the wall as Eric's wolf jumped out of the way. I glanced around, searching for the shooter, but I saw no one. Whoever was doing this was outside the temple looking in and was a damn good shot. And their bullets had to be laced with magic if they could take out vamps.

Damien stood near the door, flinging balls of magic at Bernadetta's blurring shape. She weaved in and out of the pews, trying to get to him while his hands danced in the air with grace and speed, crafting spells that conjured magic strong enough to stop one of the most powerful vampires in the city.

It was a sight to behold.

Drawing my gaze from their battle, I scanned my surroundings, searching for another target. Immediately, I homed in on Stephen Erikson who was carefully inching his way toward the door, hugging the jade cup close to his chest.

You'll pay for this, you coward.

Leaping over the vampire's body at my paws, I rushed toward Stephen, threading through the chaos of broken pews and fighting shapes to get to him. He noticed me just as he was about to sneak past Damien and Bernadetta. Pausing for a moment, he gave me a crooked smile, then pointed at me.

"Stop her," he ordered, and too late I noticed that the hybrid Bernadetta had created was trailing behind him, slinking in the shadows.

The hybrid stepped forward and let out a deafening roar as his body began to shift, his muscles rippling, his head enlarging to three times its normal size, his bones elongating and cracking, his clothes ripping. I waited for him to fall forward to all fours, but he remained standing, his features only half wolf. Fur grew sparsely over his body, pulsing, black veins visible under it. They also covered his face in a jagged road map, climbing over his partially elongated snout and slightly pointed ears, creating a web around his all-black eyes.

He was monstrous and terrifying and blocked my way as Stephen snuck past the door and ran out of the temple.

That cowardly bastard. He would pay for this.

With a guttural growl, the beast charged, a savage expression shaping his face.

I glanced right and left as what felt like a freight train headed my way. I was paralyzed for a moment, unsure of what to do. When he was only a few yards away, the hybrid fell to his hands and pressed forward, able to run both as a human and wolf.

He leaped, his hands outstretched. His fingers were long with huge knuckles and three-inch claws at their tips. I tried to move out of the way, but he was fast. His claws raked over my side, digging deep. I yelped in pain. Blood slicked my fur, quickly oozing out and dribbling down my front leg.

The creature pivoted on a dime despite his size and, this time, went for my eyes. I lowered my head just in time and charged him. I closed my jaws around his forearm and bit as hard as I could. He roared and, jerking his arm, sent me soaring across the room. I landed on top of a pew, my spine hitting it hard, cracking painfully. I rolled off and hit the floor. I tried to get up, but my legs gave and I fell again. The hybrid appeared above me, standing on top of the pew, peering down on me. He smiled with relish, a grotesque gesture in his semi-human face.

I tried to move again, but my legs wouldn't respond.

The creature dropped from the pew and caged me between his legs and arms. He lowered his snout to my ear. His throat rumbled as he inhaled deeply.

"You smell delicious," he said in a voice that was barely human and sounded more like the rumbling of stone against stone.

Rage flared inside of me. This creature was an abomination worse than any other. Why would Bernadetta and Stephen create something like this? Why couldn't they be content with what they had? Weren't immortality, heightened senses and speed, and eternal health enough? Why couldn't they let everyone live in peace?

The hybrid's fangs grew larger still, sliding out with a wet sound. He angled his head as I commanded my body to stand and fight, but I felt nothing. My spine was broken.

As he moved closer, angling his mouth to my neck, I shook my head on reflex, and realized that I could move at least that much. Focusing on his arm, which he was using to keep himself propped up above me, I thrust my head forward, clamped my teeth around it, and bit with all my strength, willing all my rage into him.

Energy coursed through my body and seemed to spill through my mouth right into the hybrid. He let out a strangled cry, throwing his head backward. A flash of light went through his body for an instant, then he fell on top of me, his heavy body limp and smothering.

I listened for his breath and heartbeat but got nothing. Had *I* killed him? Or had the blood from the dagger done that? I had no way of knowing.

The battle went on around me. Magic flashed on and off like strobe lights. Growls and roars resonated against the stone walls. Crashing sounds, moans of pain, shattering glass.

Get up. Get up.

I kept trying to move, but I couldn't feel my body from the neck down.

Please, please, let me be all right.

All of a sudden, I went from feeling nothing to experiencing a flash of pain traveling across my spine. I shuddered, my entire body convulsing. Sensation returned in stages, my limbs tingling, my back screaming in agony. My every nerve ending was on fire.

The pain went on for an eternity or a few minutes, I couldn't tell which, but I welcomed it because it was better than feeling nothing. Even as the pain droned on, sensation returned to my limbs, and I could move them again.

Holy witchlights! Had I just recovered from spinal injury? Had my back knit itself back together? Either way, I couldn't be more thankful for being a werewolf and having healing abilities.

Cringing from pain, I moved from under the hybrid and slowly rose up on trembling legs. I glanced around, surveying the chaos.

Damien was still fighting, doing his best to keep Bernadetta at bay. Sweat shone on his brow, and he seemed to be tiring, but not Bernadetta. She was still attacking, trying to get to him while magical attacks rained on her.

Some of his volleys grazed her, but they barely managed to send her skidding back, her boots scraping against the stone floor. Once, he managed to hit her straight on, and she went flying against the wall, but she immediately got back up and doggedly launched for the mage again. She intended to tire him, and it was working.

I was trying to figure out what to do when Jake and Eric joined me, one standing at each side. I glanced around and realized they were the only ones left standing. No one else was fighting, and the shots had stopped. It seemed we'd taken the rest of the vampires down. But what about the werewolf captives? I spotted a couple of them on the floor, licking their wounds. Were the other ones dead? I turned my face away, refusing to look.

I saw you go down, Eric's voice sounded inside my head. *Are you all right?"*

I am, but Damien… he's tiring.

He glanced over at Jake, and a silent message seemed to pass between them. Together, they moved toward the Dark Donna, prowling, stalking. I joined them. Jake glanced sideways at me, and I expected him to tell me to stay back, but he only gave a nod.

Apparently, he was starting to realize I could take care of myself.

We formed a circle around Bernadetta. Damien noticed us, and I thought I saw a twitch of relief pass his features. At last, the vamp stopped moving and glanced around. Her black eyes regarded us one at a time as if assessing the threat we each posed. Something changed in her expression after she finished doing the math. The numbers didn't add up in her favor. She was strong, but not three alphas and one Copper Mage strong.

She hissed in frustration and let her gaze dart around the room.

Eric advanced, his hackles raised, his fangs bared. His wolf wasn't nearly as large as Jake's, but there was a certain edge to the way he moved that drove fear under my skin and made me go cold inside.

Jake and I took Eric's lead and inched closer. Damien weaved a spell in the air, his lips moving silently. We had her surrounded, and this was our chance to take her down. After that, we'd only have Stephen to worry about, and I doubted he would be hard to take down. Though maybe I was wrong. Weasels could be pretty tricky.

Eric lunged toward the vamp first. Jake went next, and I followed. Moving faster than the eye can see, the Dark Donna jumped into the air and hovered out of reach, looking down on us with contempt as we jumped on our hind legs, snarling and teeth snapping in our failed attempts to reach her.

Damien's attack came next. A crackling blob of magic the size of a basketball hit Bernadetta in the chest, exploding with blue light. She flew upward, tumbling head over heels, and crashed against the wall. I expected her to fall, but instead, she clung to the stones, her claws digging in.

Damien set to working on another spell, and we ran toward the wall to wait for her fall. But before the mage could release another volley, the Dark Donna crawled upward like a spider, and with her bare hands tore away a section of roof, and crept out of sight, leaving us dodging the falling roof tiles and staring at a sliver of moon through a ragged hole.

A moment later, quick steps echoed outside the church. I whirled expecting to see the Dark Donna charging back in for another battle. Instead, I watched with my jaw hanging open as Rosalina rushed in, wearing a badass leather outfit, a rifle with a huge scope slung over her shoulder.

"Is it over?" she asked. "Did we win?"

Shut the front door!

I gaped, seriously starting to doubt I'd healed from my spinal injury. Maybe I was still under the hybrid, lost in feverish delirium because I knew Rosalina wasn't a leather-wearing, scope-rifle-toting badass.

And if I was wrong, then the world had really gone mad.

CHAPTER 31

The next evening, everyone was crammed in the tiny lobby at the agency. Me, Rosalina, Jake, Damien, and even Eric Lone himself.

There was a metal bucket filled with ice on top of Rosalina's desk, and a nice bottle of champagne that Eric had provided. I had bought clear plastic cups that looked like wine glasses and a tray of hors d'oeuvres that included tiny quiche pies, cold cuts, and bite-sized crab cakes.

"We make a kickass team," I said, picking up the bottle and raising it high.

Damien shrugged one shoulder and sat on the small sofa, gathering his cloak to one side and setting his top hat on the coffee table.

Eric joined him and sat, crossing his leg. "Fill my cup to the brim, please."

I huffed. "Fill it yourself!"

Trying to have a celebration with this bunch was sad.

I poured myself some bubbly and paraded in front of Eric,

sipping the champagne and making pleasure sounds in the back of my throat.

"Women these days," Damien said, rolling his copper eyes.

"This is not the eighteen hundreds, grandpa." Rosalina got her own champagne and, after tasting it, said, "good choice."

"Grandpa?" Damien said, sounding offended. "I'm nobody's grandpa, and, for your information, I wasn't born in the eighteen hundreds."

Rosalina made a dismissive gesture with her hand. "You were born around 1905 or thereabouts, so same difference."

The mage's eyes narrowed, and he didn't argue, which probably meant that was a close guess.

Jake poured his own champagne, too. He knew better than anyone that expecting me to play the dutiful female was pressing all the wrong buttons. I was glad to do something for anyone as long as I didn't feel they were taking advantage of me or being sexist. Otherwise, I turned hostile. In my opinion, everyone had to pull their own weight.

But enough of that. I wanted to celebrate that we were alive and that we'd stopped Bernadetta and Stephen's evil scheme and there were no hybrid monsters loose in the city.

After our battle, we had all left the temple, taking the couple of werewolves who were still alive with us. Damien had patched up their worst injuries, doing a fairly good job despite the fact that he wasn't a healer. We offered to take them to a hospital afterward, but they just wanted to get as far away from St. Louis as they could. The ordeal had left them terrified as well as *packless*. It turned out that the ten werewolves had all belonged to a small pack that occupied a reduced territory outside the city limits, and they had nothing to go back to.

Afterward, we'd anonymously called the police. The massacre at the temple would raise a lot of questions from law enforcement, and they would be looking for someone to blame for all those deaths. To the law, murder was murder, and we would all end up in jail for the deaths of those vampires whether or not we had good reason for killing them. Thankfully, Damien seemed to be an expert at removing evidence from crime scenes, and he assured us there was no way they would be able to trace the chaos back to us in any shape or form.

It had been a night I would never forget.

Begrudgingly, Eric stood from the couch and poured himself some champagne. He licked his lips after the first sip, then poured more in his cup, and pestered me with the same question he'd already asked me twice today. "Are you sure the dagger is safe, Sunder?"

"Yes! It is!" *Sheesh.*

"I won't feel at ease until the Pack Rule has it in its possession," he said.

"Maybe it's safer with me," I said. "Have you thought about that? Huh?"

Eric gave me a look that seemed to ask *"What are you smoking?"*

I sighed in irritation. "What if one of those stuffy Rule dudes gets ideas and decides to put the dagger to *good use*?"

"They won't do that. They'll keep it safe."

"Since when do you trust them?" Damien asked.

Eric glared at the mage.

"He just doesn't trust *me* 'cause I'm just a pup," I said.

"I agree with Eric," Jake said. "I'll breathe a lot easier when it's out of your hands."

I rolled my eyes. But of course.

"Bernadetta or Stephen could come looking for it, Toni." Jake's tone sounded like something he should use on a child, not me.

"I'm not afraid of them," I said. "Let them come, then I'll show them a dagger." I lifted my middle finger, letting a sharp claw spring out.

To my surprise, Eric laughed a full belly laugh, something I'd never heard from him. Damien surreptitiously smiled at his friend, looking pleased to see him so merry.

Eric caught his breath and returned to his seat, champagne in hand. "The Pack Rule meets in only three days, I guess I can trust the pup that long." He gave me a friendly wink.

In all honesty, I wasn't *that* confident about keeping the dagger. Stephen didn't worry me, but the Dark Donna was another story. More than anything, I was counting on their assumption that I wouldn't be so stupid as to keep the dagger. If anything, they would probably guess Damien had it, and he could hold his own against Bernadetta.

Pushing those gloomy thoughts aside, I turned to Rosalina and clinked my glass to hers. "I still can't believe you have been training behind my back. You turned into a regular Black Widow or something."

She gave me a cheeky smile and winked. "I was tired of being left behind all the time, and *you* getting to see all the action."

"Yes, but what about all your common sense and sensibility?"

"I threw them out the window." She pretended to throw something over her shoulder.

"It doesn't sound anything like you."

Her expression sobered. "I know. I guess I was just afraid."

I frowned. "What do you mean?"

"Afraid to lose my best friend," she said, her dark eyes locking with mine.

I opened my mouth to argue, but she didn't let me speak.

"And don't try to tell me I wouldn't lose you because, the way things are going, there are two ways for that to happen. One, you decide that running this agency is boring and fighting crime is more exciting. Or two, you get killed because I wasn't there to protect you."

I didn't know what to say to that. I guessed I should've realized she would feel this way even if she was partly wrong.

"I could always get killed," I said. "There's no shortage of buses in the city, and I could always get hit by one of them, but I would never be bored of our agency. I love working with you. I'm excited to wake up every morning and come here to work with my best friend."

"Really?"

"Of course." I wrapped her in a tight hug. I didn't like this idea of her running around like a vigilante, no matter how badass she'd become with a rifle, but if I was going to jump into danger whenever it called my name, I had no right to tell her not to do the same.

When we pulled away from each other, I noticed Damien regarding my friend over the rim of his cup. He had used his magic to fetch himself a serving of champagne and was sitting back comfortably while he admired Rosalina's beauty from afar.

"Someone's checking you out," I said out of the corner of my mouth.

She took a sip of bubbly, blinking lazily at the mage, using all her drool-inducing, female guiles on him. He pushed to the edge of the sofa, unable to resist.

"Hmm, I need more champagne," I said, even though my cup was half-full.

Jake was halfway sitting on Rosalina's desk, one leg up and the other still firmly on the floor. After I refilled my cup, I stood in front of him and gave him a once over. His faded jeans hugged his powerful thighs, making me want to run my hands along their muscular length. He wore a dark gray button-up shirt rolled up to the elbows, and his favorite biker boots. They were black, square-toed with one inch heels and several scuff marks. A row of leather bracelets wrapped around his left wrist. Something new to replace the bracelet he'd given me.

"Why didn't you tell me you were training Rosalina?"

"Because she asked me not to."

Rosalina had gone to Jake after the rhabo incident at the Pulse Inc. warehouse, and he'd been teaching her all about weapons and self-defense ever since.

"Like I told you," Jake said, "she's a natural. I've taught her all I could, but I've referred her to a buddy of mine because she's eager to learn more. She also wants to learn how to wield a sword."

"What?!"

"Yep."

"What has gotten into her?"

"Maybe she's an adrenaline junkie, and she never knew."

More than ever, we needed to get back to just tracking mates. If we didn't, at this rate, we would end up joining a SWAT team or something.

Another thing that Jake had done behind my back was put a tracker in the bracelet he'd given me. That was how they'd found me at the temple. A tracker on a tracker, wasn't that ironic? Rosalina had known about it, and when I hadn't answered her calls, she'd contacted Jake, who traced the signal to the temple. I fiddled with it for a moment, then set the glass down and tried to undo the clasp.

Jake wrapped a hand around my wrist, trapping the bracelet. "No, please, keep it."

I shook my head. "It doesn't feel right."

"It saved your life."

That, it had, but I didn't want him knowing where I was 24/7.

He seemed to read my thoughts because he said, "I won't use it to track you unless I think you're in danger."

I jutted my hip out. "What if I'm on a hot date?"

His silver eyes darken, pupils growing wide. "Please don't."

"Don't what? Go on a date?"

He blinked once in response.

"Fine for you to say, *Mr. Engaged.*"

"I'm working on it," he said in a low whisper. "I made you a promise."

"That doesn't mean I can't have fun while you do."

A sad smile stretched his chiseled lips. "I'm not having any fun, I assure you."

"You expect me to believe Ms. Allison Blackridge doesn't try to enjoy her fiancé."

"Believe it or not, we hardly talk."

Well, that was nothing like what I'd been imagining. When I met her at Walter Knight's house, I'd gotten a different impression. Of course, I had been blinded by jealousy, so there was no telling which of my memories were real and which were enhanced by my envy of her.

"What? Is she shy or something?" I asked.

"I don't think so." He looked pensive for a moment. "She's just a victim of the circumstances as much as me."

That certainly offered a different perspective that I hadn't considered. This was an arranged marriage, and though it was not unheard of among werewolves, it wasn't common either. Still, she'd had to agree, right? Jake had. No one had forced him. Of course, he was a strong alpha, and I doubted anyone could force him to do anything he didn't want. Allison, on the other hand… She wasn't an alpha, from what I understood. Maybe they *had* forced her.

I frowned. I knew better than to get my hopes up. This pact between the Blackridges and the Knights was real.

"Either way," I shrugged. "You got yourself into this mess, and even though I'll be waiting, I don't see why I shouldn't have a little fun in the meantime."

"Because you love me." Jake grinned his heart-stopping grin.

It was true enough. He was the only man I'd ever loved, but was it smart to put my life on hold for him, hoping he *might* get out of an unbreakable pact?

I turned away from Jake, determined not to lose my good humor, and grabbed a miniature quiche from the hors d'oeuvres tray. As I nibbled on it, I noticed Damien finally standing from the couch and walking toward Rosalina.

He gave her a tentative smile, and they began talking, their gazes furtively meeting, then falling to the floor. I smiled, glad to see that Damien had gotten over that call to the police. If I was objective about it, I realized that it wasn't a minor offense. If someone called the police on me, I wasn't so sure I could forgive them at all. But obviously, Damien was a better person than me and willing to look past that stumbling block.

Everything was looking up. Tomorrow Josh's antidote would be ready. Damien would save his daughter, and we would save our customer and possibly our reputation.

ꙮ

The next day after a leisurely lunch with Rosalina at one of our favorite restaurants, we got back to the office to wait for Damien. To pass the time, I went in the potions alcove to gather ingredients and make sure I had everything I needed for our new customer.

I lost track of time and, glancing at my phone, I walked out into the lobby. “Damien is late,” I said.

Rosalina glanced up from the computer and checked her wrist watch, frowning. “Yeah, that’s unlike him. Should I call?” She reached for her phone.

“Maybe. Or just send him a text.”

Her thumbs moved quickly over the screen, then she hit send. She was putting the phone down when the front door burst open, and the mage staggered into the room, then collapsed to the floor.

“Damien!” Rosalina exclaimed, jumping to her feet.

We both ran to him and knelt by his side. Damien was laying on his stomach. We grabbed his shoulders and helped him roll over.

Rosalina gasped. I pressed a hand to my mouth.

A large hole was carved in his chest, the edges glowing with crackling magic, bones and sinew visible.

Oh, no! Dread washed over me.

“Call 911!” Rosalina exclaimed.

I reached for my phone and dialed quickly. I talked to the dispatcher and gave her directions to the agency.

Rosalina’s hands hovered over Damien’s chest, her face contorting as she seemed to run through things she could do to help and came up blank.

“You’ll be all right,” she said. “Someone will be here soon to help you.”

I pulled at my hair, wishing I had some of my sister’s healing abilities so I could help Damien. I took his hand in mine, my heart pounding out of control.

“Who did this?” I asked.

“M-midnight Witch,” he managed.

Of course, only a more advanced mage would’ve been able to best him.

"Do you know her?"

He shook his head and coughed, his face disfiguring in what could only be pain. Tears spilled down Rosalina's cheeks as she smoothed his white hair and gazed deep into his eyes.

"Can you heal yourself?" I asked.

"Too… weak."

Seconds ticked by. Damien's breaths grew ragged. He glanced pointedly toward his hand. It lay open and limp on the floor.

"What is it?" I asked.

He whispered a few words under his breath. A spell? Maybe he had enough strength to try to heal himself, after all. When he was done, he exhaled in relief.

"T-the cure," he murmured.

I frowned and glanced toward his hand again. Two small vials that hadn't been there before now rested on his palm. They shimmered with a clear liquid. They were accompanied by the coin-shaped carving he'd used to go gain passage to Elf-hame.

"Make sure… my daughter gets the cure. Please. She must drink it all."

I shook my head. "You'll give it to her yourself." My voice wavered with emotion, my hope slipping away.

"Promise." He moved his hand a fraction to recall my attention to the vials.

I carefully took them and the token from his palm and stored them securely in the breast pocket of my jacket. "I promise."

His entire body seemed to exhale with relief.

"The token is for you."

I would've argued about him giving me something so valuable, but I didn't have the heart, so I just nodded.

He turned to Rosalina.

"I wish… things would've turned out differently."

Rosalina pressed a hand to his cheek and smiled tenderly, then leaned forward and pressed a kiss to his pale lips. His eyes closed, and his life slipped away.

"Me, too." Rosalina rested her forehead on his shoulders and cried.

WWW.INGRIDSEYMOUR.COM

www.ingramcontent.com/pod-product-compliance
Lightning Source LLC
Chambersburg PA
CBHW020334310726
48979CB00015B/2371/J